The woman awoke with a scream building in her throat

She looked up at the samurai and saw only his long hair, dark skin and the braided leather headband. No doubt thinking that she was about to be assaulted by one of the Apache, she bit Ki's hand and her scream filled the air.

Ki spun on his heel and his thin *tantō* blade flashed once, burying itself into the chest of the man who had claimed this woman. The other Apache seemed to spring off the ground and attack with bloodcurdling screams.

The *han-kei* whirred in a deadly circle and as the warriors threw themselves at Ki, the heavy wooden sticks smashed heads, arms, and faces. Apache warriors reeled in pain as the samurai took the fight directly to them and the *han-kei* did exactly what it had been designed centuries ago in Japan to do—knock men senseless. One Apache, smarter than his peers, grabbed a rifle and brought it up to fire, but a foot-strike to his midsection sent the warrior reeling and the whirring *han-kei* soon found and broke his skull like a thin eggshell.

Also in the LONE STAR series
from Jove

WESLEY ELLIS

LONE STAR

AND THE
ARIZONA STRANGLER

JOVE BOOKS, NEW YORK

LONE STAR AND THE ARIZONA STRANGLER

A Jove Book / published by arrangement with
the author

PRINTING HISTORY
Jove edition / November 1989

ISBN: 0-515-10174-5

PRINTED IN THE UNITED STATES OF AMERICA

10 9 8 7 6 5 4 3 2 1

Chapter 1

Jessica Starbuck was seated in her late father's study, pouring over the earnings and expense statements of her worldwide Starbuck enterprises when someone tapped lightly on her door.

"Miss Starbuck?"

Jessie turned from the massive oak desk and saw her foreman, Ed Wright. Ed had been her foreman on the Circle Star Ranch for many years and when she was frequently away from her huge Texas cattle ranch on business, Ed was in charge. He was tall, a little shy and very, very good at his job.

"Come on in," Jessie said. "I'm looking for an excuse to take a minute from these accounts."

Ed removed his hat as he entered the room, though it wasn't necessary. It was just that he was raised a gentleman, and in Texas a cowboy removed his hat when he entered the ranch house. "Sorry to disturb you, but this envelope came in by special messenger.

It's marked confidential and urgent and I just thought you'd want to see it at once."

Jessie reached for the envelope, saying, "It's probably just some beleaguered manager wanting more funds or some such thing, and the *confidential* means he'd rather not have anyone else know he's in need of funds beyond his annual budget. I'll bet the word *urgent* doesn't mean anything, either. Everyone is using it these days."

"Well, this one is from Yuma, Arizona," Ed told her. "And I know you don't have any companies down in that country. Too blamed hot and dry for cattle. About the only thing it's good for is raisin' rattlers, lizards, scorpions, and them durned old Gila monsters."

Jessie opened the envelope and pulled out a sheet of expensive notepaper and a letter that was sealed with a wax stamp.

"I got some cowboys waiting outside," Ed told her. "So if you don't need anything else, I'll get back to work."

Jessie did not hear him because she was already reading the envelope.

Dear Miss Jessica Starbuck:
My husband has been strangled to death! It was murder and I fear for my own life. Perhaps his sealed letter will explain. Please help me.
                              Mrs. Cassandra Hastings.

"Miss Starbuck, are you all right!"

Jessie bit her lip and nodded. "Yes," she said. "Please go find Ki and bring him to me at once."

"He went out before daylight, and you know he can't be found unless he wants to be. But I'll find him. Anything I can help with? All the color just drained out of your face just now."

Jessie tore her eyes from the note. "A very

dear man that I almost married has been . . . has been strangled to death in Yuma. He was the county prosecutor. His wife thinks her life may also be in grave danger by strangulation.''

"Holy cow! What kind of a man would go around strangling his enemies?''

"A very, very sick man.''

Ed nodded. He was tall, with a prominent Adam's apple and thinning hair. His face was nut brown from his eyebrows down, but his forehead was very pale because he always wore a hat except in Jessie's presence. "I'll find Ki,'' he said, backing out of the study. "Don't you worry. Have a brandy to calm your nerves. I'll be back real soon.''

Jessie listened to Ed's boots as they hurried down the polished hallway and then across the porch. A moment later she heard her foreman giving orders to his crew to spread out and ride fast looking for the samurai.

For several long minutes Jessie stared at the sealed letter with a rising sense of apprehension. She thought of Warren Hastings, and when she closed her eyes she could almost see his handsome face. Once, he had loved her very much, and had it not been for his pride that forbade him to marry the daughter of a very rich man, he'd have proposed. Instead, Jessie's heart had nearly broken when she received the news that he was leaving Texas and going to Arizona. Within six months after his arrival in Yuma, he had been appointed county prosecutor and had married a widow, Mrs. Cassandra Potter, now Mrs. Cassandra Hastings and . . . God help her poor suffering soul, again, a widow.

Jessie used a silver letter opener to pry away the wax seal, and she read Warren's letter, dated only ten days earlier.

3

Dear Miss Jessica:

I write this letter with great anxiety and concern because I fear my life is about to end. The circumstances for this deduction are too elaborate to outline at this moment, but suffice to say that I am being stalked by a madman. A diabolical beast who has killed often and never with any weapon save a garrote. The idea of being strangled fills me with pure terror. I am not the first man to know such fears and my exhaustive research has turned up no less than seven other unfortunate victims—judges, prosecuting attorneys such as myself, and two sheriffs—all mysteriously strangled to death. Tacked to my office door, I found a crude drawing of a man hanging in death, face blackened, tongue protruding grotesquely from his mouth, eyes bulged in horror. I am almost beside myself with fear. The list of suspects grows daily and rests in my safe to be used by you and Ki in the event of my death in order to bring to justice the fiend that the press is already describing as the Arizona Strangler. I have no one else to turn to for help. Please hurry west on the very next stage and . . . God help me . . . if you are too late, please protect my dear Cassandra.

Sincerely,
Warren Hastings,
your devoted admirer and friend

Jessie placed the letter down and reached for a quill and began to write a letter for her secretary to duplicate and send to her companies worldwide. In the letter were instructions that her correspondence be held until she returned from urgent business in Yuma. She finished the letter, rang for her secretary, and instructed him to duplicate the letter and finish handling the remaining stack of her mail with apologies to those for whom a delay would cause real inconvenience.

"But Miss Starbuck," the older man mildly protested. "Surely a trip to Yuma, Arizona, would be better scheduled for the winter months. This being July, it will be hotter than . . . than blazes!"

"And hell," Jessie said. "Yes, I know that, but this is a matter of great urgency and I have to go now. Do you remember Mr. Hastings?"

"Of course! A fine young man."

"He's been murdered and his wife fears her own life is in danger," Jessie said. "I have to see what can be done to help."

"But can't you simply send for the woman? We have plenty of room here at the Circle Star and—"

"No," Jessie said. "Not if the Arizona Strangler is to be captured."

The secretary, a gentle but very conscientious and efficent man in his late fifties, nodded. "Just be careful. Please."

"I'm taking Ki," Jessie said.

The secretary relaxed. "I was sure you would and will rest much easier now. We all will here at the Circle Star."

"So will I." Jessie headed down the hallway toward her room to pack. The huge ranch house was cool and dim inside with its thick adobe walls and high beamed ceilings, and Jessie's stride was long and smooth, like her figure. She was a beauty even in the denim pants that showed the firm roundness of her buttocks and accentuated her narrow waist over perfectly rounded hips. Her eyes were green and they could flash when she was angry. Her hair was honey-blond, and her breasts pressed enticingly against the western shirts that she favored.

Jessie, like her late father, Alex Starbuck, could have lived anywhere in the world, but chose this Texas cattle ranch. It was as much a part of her as her bones, and both she and Alex had planned to live here forever. In Alex's case, forever had come sooner than anyone had expected.

Jessie paused in the hallway to contemplate a charcoal sketch of her late father. It was the one that had been drawn by a close friend right after Alex had bought his first seagoing vessel. What a day that must have been! Jessie could almost hear him relate again how he'd started out in life as a very small importer and exporter of Oriental furniture and quality antiques. He had opened his doors in a little shop in San Francisco, but soon he had expanded his business to the point where he needed a ship to import his own products. One ship had become many over the next few years, and Alex Starbuck had been the first to use iron-hulled vessels and convert from sail to steam. By the time he was in his mid-forties, the Starbuck legend was already being made in many isolated corners of the world.

Alex had not been greedy, but his thirst for new enterprises and challenges had been unquenchable. He had gotten into rubber plantations in South and Central America, diamond mines in South Africa, oil, and finally steel to build not only his own huge fleet of ships, but also for railroad tracks. Everything he touched had turned to gold.

Jessie smiled at the sketch. "I would have rather you lived to be an old, crotchety man than a rich one who died too young," she said. She passed on to her room, thinking about how Alex had finally been murdered by an international cartel of pirates and corporate sharks who had made a bold attempt to destroy the world economy through the collapse of its banking system. To do that, they'd needed Alex Starbuck's power and money. They had offered him wealth beyond measure, and when he'd declined, they'd elected to take his life. Instead, they had bungled the job and instead taken Jessie's mother's

6

life in what the European authorities still believed had been an accident when an out of control carriage had struck them while crossing a cobblestone street.

Jessie had been too young to understand or to grieve too long. But Alex had never quite recovered from the loss of his wife, and he had fought the cartel with renewed determination until they'd finally succeeded in murdering him right here on the Circle Star, where he'd always felt his safety was assured.

Inside her room, Jessie packed with practiced efficiency. By the time she was finished, Ki was standing at her door.

"I am ready," the samurai said, not troubling her with questions that he knew she would answer when there was more time.

"Good." Jessie removed her six-gun, holster, and cartidge belt from her drawer and strapped it to her hip. "Did Ed tell you anything?"

"A little." The samurai folded his arms across his chest and stood watching her. He was the son 'of an American sailor and a Japanese princess, and genetics had blessed him with the finest physical and emotional characteristics of both races. Ki had inherited his father's height and stood just under six feet tall. His shoulders were much broader than that of most Japanese men, but his eyes were dark and almond-shaped. He had lived as an orphan in Japan after his father and mother had died in separate tragedies, and Jessie knew that he had almost starved to death before being befriended by an old *rōnin*. *Rōnin* meant "wave man," and in the Land of the Rising Sun, a samurai who had no master was thought of as one whose life was blown hither and yon like a leaf to the wind or the froth of a wave on a high and storm-tossed sea. A *rōnin* was a man without a purpose, a poor creature whose very existence was unworthy of consideration by those more fortunate.

7

A *rōnin* had nothing, was nothing, would never be anything. Such a man had found meaning in the life of a small, starving boy. A boy who, to the Japanese way of thinking, was a creature more unworthy than a dog. A boy who was the product of a mixed marriage between a Japanese woman of royal blood and a hated foreigner.

When Jessie was finished packing, Ki came inside and took her suitcase. "Ed has a carriage ready for us. We will be traveling across Apache country?"

"Yes," Jessie told him. "And just a few weeks ago I heard that the Apache were raising hell down in the Sonoran Desert."

"Is it wise to go that way?"

"No," Jessie said. "But it's the most expedient way, and we are on a mission of great urgency. We just don't have the time to loop north through Santa Fe and hope for an army escort."

"Ed Wright and your men want to come."

"They can't be spared right now," Jessie said. "The range is dry and it's all they can do to keep the cattle moving to pastures with water and some feed. No, I can't ask Ed to pull his men off the ranges for us."

"We will reach Yuma safely," the samurai promised.

Jessie looked up into his dark eyes and felt sure that he would help bring her through any danger that might await them between her ranch and Yuma. Ki was not a huge man or even an imposing one. But he was brave, resourceful, and the most skilled fighter she had ever known. He could kill, maim, or simply render harmless anyone that threatened them.

Even the Apache. He'd proven that before, and if they struck the stage, he'd prove it all over again.

They were on a stagecoach by eight o'clock that evening and rolling westward toward old El Paso.

Between them and El Paso were dangers, and the Comanche were still raiding, but the stagecoach had two shotgun guards and Jessie did not expect trouble.

Besides herself and Ki were an inebriated drummer named Barnaby Benjamin; a plain but pleasant woman in her thirties who was going west to Fort Yuma to be reunited with her husband, a master sergeant; and a brash young freighter who had a job in El Paso and could not keep his eyes off the prominent swells of Jessie's bosom.

The drummer sat across from Jessie and he also kept looking at her, though Jessie was doubtful that the man was capable of focusing his eyes. After about twenty miles the drummer finished nipping at his bottle, burped crudely, and said, "Excuse me, miss. But I never thought I'd see the day when a lady like you would have to sit next to a damned Chinaman."

Jessie had been looking out the window, but now she turned and regarded the drummer with coldness. "Ki is my friend and he is not a Chinaman. His father was an American and his mother was a Japanese princess. So I guess that makes his lineage a little more pedigreed than either yours or mine, wouldn't you agree?"

The drummer looked into Ki's eyes and his most basic preservational instincts, despite been dulled by alcohol, caused him to straighten in his seat and nod his head. "Meant no insult, miss. It's just that he just sits there like a cigar-store wooden Indian. I was wondering if he was a mute."

"No, Mr. Benjamin, he is very articulate. It's only that he doesn't waste his breath on drunken fools. It's an example I intend to follow from this moment until the one that you are displaced from this coach."

The drummer shifted uncomfortably. He tried to work up some righteous outrage at the insult, but he

9

kept glancing at the stern-faced samurai and was unnerved.

The young freighter sneered, "Hell, Mr. Benjamin, ain't you got no spine? You just been royally insulted. Now, I reckon you deserve that, but you sure don't have to kowtow to this half-breed Celestial sonofabitch."

Ki's hand was a blur as it traveled less than eighteen inches across the middle of the coach and delivered a stunning knife-hand chop to the base of the young freighter's neck. The man had tried to react but had been much too slow and now, as his eyes crossed and he slumped over against the door, Ki said, "I noticed he has been staring at you, Jessie. The next stage station is only a few miles back; don't you agree he needs some fresh air?"

Jessie nodded. "Yes, I do."

Ki opened the door, grabbed the freighter by the shirtfront, and hurled him out into the night.

"My Lord!" cried the sergeant's wife, whose name was Mrs. Wakefield. "He might have broken his neck in that fall!"

"Yes," Ki said. "On the other hand, he might also have learned a very important lesson in good manners. One that will keep him from getting shot and killed by someone the next time he curses in the company of ladies."

Mrs. Wakefield closed her mouth and nodded her head in slow agreement. "You are absolutely correct, Mr. Ki. My husband is not a profane man except when he is thrown by a horse or bit by a mule. There is, however, all too much profanity on an army post. And I fear that, if you attempt to re-educate every man who cusses in front of Miss Starbuck, you shall soon be overpowered and knocked quite silly. If not by the first man you reprimand, then by the one soon after."

10

"Ki is a samurai," Jessie explained. "That is a man who fights with both his hands and his feet."

Mrs. Wakefield raised her eyebrows. "And I can see he is quite good at that. But what use are hands and feet against a man with a gun or knife? Or even worse, God forbid, the Apache with their weapons. You know, they're armed with rifles now. No more bows and arrows. Mr. Wakefield warns me that some of them even have repeaters. That's better weaponry than those darned old Sharps carbines that he's issued."

The woman looked so concerned that Jessie forced a smile and said, "I realize that it must be hard on the wife of an enlisted man at such a desolate fort as the one in Yuma."

"It's a terrible life," Mrs. Wakefield confided. "It's so hot during half the year that you can fry eggs on the compound and you can iron clothes without starting a fire to heat your iron. It's a caste system all across the frontier. If you're an officer—even one wet behind the ears and fresh out of West Point—you can hardly do any wrong. But if you're a career man like my Arnold and love the army, they'll still treat you and your family worse than the lowest form of niggers or greasers."

Jessie did not approve of those terms and yet they were used constantly along the frontier. Especially the term *greaser*, which the Anglos used in a derogatory manner to describe the Mexicans. The term had originated from the fact that, after the Civil War, many of the displaced Mexicans had lost their jobs to Anglo cowboys and were considered fit only to boil the carcasses of the wild cattle and to make and sell tallow, which was the dirtiest, the greasiest job imaginable. Jessie, however, employed many Mexicans on her great Circle Star Ranch, and her vaqueros were without peer when it came to riding and roping. They were soft-spoken, fun-loving, and

11

as loyal as any group of men that had ever ridden for a brand.

The drummer could not seem to take his eyes off the samurai. Finally Ki turned his attention to the man and said, "You seem to have a questioning look on your face. Is there some mystery that you'd like answered?"

"Yeah. How'd you do it?"

"What?"

"Knock that fella out using just the edge of your hand."

"It was really not very difficult," Ki said, stiffening his hand and raising it toward the drummer. "Allow me to demonstrate."

"No! Please. I'm not *that* interested."

"Then study the ceiling of this coach or look out the window," Ki said. "Before I help you take a long nap."

The drummer nodded his head rapidly. Mrs. Wakefield stifled a smile, and Jessie shook her head with amusement as the coach rolled on toward El Paso and then the blistering and often deadly Sonoran Desert.

Chapter 2

Their trip on to El Paso was gratefully uneventful. When they arrived in that southwestern city, the temperature was over a hundred degrees in the shade and the horses as well as the driver and guards were almost overcome with heat. El Paso was sizzling, and the driver barely managed to crawl down from his seat to utter, "We won't leave until after dark when it cools down some, Miss Starbuck. You can kill both men and horses in this kind of weather."

Jessie did not argue the point. It had been stifling in the coach and, for the last two hundred miles, they had been plagued by a very fine dust that defied every attempt to keep it outside. The dust reacted to human skin like alkali and caused everyone's skin creases to abrade and turn reddish with irritation.

"We'll be staying at the Cattleman's Hotel," Jessie said. "Mrs. Wakefield, would you care to join us inside? We can have a glass of cold tea, and I'm sure that you'd feel very refreshed."

The woman was standing in the dust holding a rather large satchel and looking around as if she were lost. Jessie knew better, however, and suspected that the woman was searching for her sergeant husband to meet her.

"No, thank you," Mrs. Wakefield said. "I'll wait for Mr. Wakefield to come for me. I sent him a letter telling him of my arrival, so he'll be here momentarily."

"But you can't just stand out here in the sun and wait for him. At least come up and sit in the shade of the hotel porch."

Mrs. Wakefield managed a smile. "All right. It wouldn't do for my husband to see me lying in the street passed out from sunstroke, now, would it?"

"No," Jessie said, taking the woman's arm. "It would not do at all."

She led Mrs. Wakefield up to the porch, then asked Ki to go inside and bring them both a glass of cold tea.

Ki had been in the Cattleman's Hotel a number of times with his boss, and he passed quickly through the lobby into a small restaurant, where he ordered the tea. "Put it on Miss Starbuck's tab," he said to the waiter who brought the glasses to him.

"Oh, is she here at this time of year?"

"It was unavoidable," Ki said. "You can be sure of that much."

The waiter was perspiring freely. "Nobody but nobody should come through this country in the summer. Me, I'm too broke to leave, and by the time I have the money for a stagecoach to California, it'll be fall and I'll decide to stay another year."

Ki took the glasses out to the two women who were seated on the porch. The samurai handed them the glasses and leaned against a porch post. Although American history was in its infancy compared to that of Japan, Ki did enjoy knowing a little something about the places that he and Jessie traveled. El Paso was a city with a rich cultural and historical heritage. It had gotten its name in the sixteenth century when the intrepid Spaniards, coming northward from Chihuahua, viewed the Rio Grande flanked by two prominent mountain ranges rising out of the desert. The river formed a deep chasm and this place the Spaniards named, El Paso del Norte. Later, the impatient Anglos simply shortened the name to El Paso. Sister city Juarez was born on the southern bank of the river a few years later. In the decades that followed, both El Paso and Juarez had grown steadily despite the harsh environment that surrounded them. They became a major crossroads, and always the Rio Grande was the life-blood of both cities. It slaked the thirst of its inhabitants, and its warm, usually muddy waters were used to irrigate field crops, primarily corn, wheat, and beans.

Periodically the Apache had attacked and even overrun El Paso, but they had never been able to hold or destroy it. El Paso, with each year, grew stronger and more independent of the Apache, so that when the Texans won their independence under Sam Houston, El Paso scarcely noted the historic event or even cared. The majority of its inhabitants were still peaceful Indians and Mexicans. With the establishment of Fort Bliss, peace and security were assured and El Paso remained comfortable in its role as a major southwestern trading center.

"My husband," Mrs. Wakefield was saying, "loves the army, and I'd never tell him that I yearn for civilian life, but it's true. Sometimes living at some primitive army post becomes such a burden on my mind that I have to get away. I always return to Georgia and visit my family. Seeing the green for-

15

ests after all this sagebrush is enough to make me weep like a ninny.''

"Is that where you've been this time?" Jessie asked, somehow managing to look cool despite the punishing heat.

"Yes. But I was reluctant to go because of the Apache trouble they've been having. I know that nothing will happen to Mr. Wakefield, but still . . . it preys on your mind."

"I'm sure he'll be along soon," Jessie said, her green eyes surveying the dusty streets and the constant stream of freight wagons that rolled past the Cattleman's Hotel. "Look, is that him?"

Mrs. Wakefield turned so quickly that she spilled her tea, but then her shoulders slumped with disappointment. "No, that is Sergeant Barling. He's a friend of my husband's and may know why he has been detained."

Sergeant Barling was a thick slab of a man, red-faced and sweating as he tromped down the street. When he saw Mrs. Wakefield, he did not smile or wave in greeting but came directly over to see her. He took a long look at Jessie and then stepped out of the sun, removed his hat, and said, "Agnes, I'm afraid I have some bad news for you."

Agnes Wakefield paled a little, then recovered to ask, "What is it?"

"Your husband has been transferred to Fort Yuma. He asked me to explain and see to it that you were taken care of and didn't go on until it was safe."

The woman visibly relaxed. "But why was he transferred?"

"Apache. You've been gone, but there's been a lot of killing between here and Yuma. The sergeant, he'd like you to stay here until the trouble is over and then go on to meet him."

"Absolutely not!"

Sergeant Barling sleeved his perspiring face dry

and scowled. "Agnes, it's what your husband wants. He says that it's too dangerous to travel right now."

"If it was too dangerous, then the stage line would cancel its run to Yuma," the woman countered. "No, I won't stay in this insufferable town another minute longer than I absolutely have to."

"You wouldn't stay here anyway. The wife and I can put you up with us. You'd be comfortable, though you know it'd be kind of crowded. Agnes, we're just talking about a couple of months."

"Out of the question!"

Sergeant Barling, his argument ignored, looked beseechingly at Jessie. "Miss, are you her friend?"

"Yes, I suppose I am. Why?"

"Well, try and talk a little sense into her for me," the sergeant said. "You heard what I just told her. Make her see that she needs to stay right here where there's no danger."

"I can hardly do that," Jessie told the soldier, "because I fully intend to go on to Yuma on this evening's stage."

The sergeant's eyes widened. "You're making a mistake about that," he said with a shake of his head. "If the Apache get ahold of you or Mrs. Wakefield, they'll do terrible things to the both of you."

Ki stepped forward. "We're aware of the dangers, Sergeant. Even so, Miss Starbuck and Mrs. Wakefield have made their decisions. They are going on. If you feel that worried, perhaps you can convince your commanding officer to provide a military escort."

"Who the devil are you?"

"He's my friend and traveling companion," Jessie said. "And he has a good suggestion. Why don't you speak to your commanding officer and ask him to send a detail of cavalrymen along with us for protection?"

"Because he'd laugh in my face," the sergeant

17

snapped. "Good heavens, ma'am! We got our hands full right here!"

"Well," Jessie said, her eyes frosting, "then I guess that about concludes our conversation."

The sergeant raked the toe of his dust-covered boot on the splintered porch and turned back to Mrs. Wakefield. "If you go and anything should happen to you, your husband will never forgive me."

"Nothing will happen," Agnes said. "Besides, what are you supposed to do, throw me in the stockade against my will? John, be easy about this. You tried your best to keep me here, but I would not listen."

"Yeah," he said, slapping his hat on and turning to go. "Just don't forget you were warned, and tell your husband I tried."

They watched the sergeant march back up the dusty street, and when he was out of hearing range, Agnes said, "I hope I'm not being foolish." She looked up at Jessie. "Am I?"

Jessie was not sure what to say. The last thing she wanted was the responsibility for making a decision that would affect another person's life.

"Agnes, if I were in your shoes, I would have made exactly the same decision you made. To wait here for months, wondering if your husband was dead or alive, well or injured—that would be a torment."

"Thank you for saying that," Agnes whispered. "Now, since I don't have to wait here for Mr. Wakefield, why don't we go inside where it's cooler?"

"Wonderful idea," Jessie said.

Ki remained outside. He pulled up an old rocking chair and propped his feet up and watched the street with more than a casual interest. He was dressed in his usual dark, loose shirt and pants, and wearing sandals, and his long black hair was held neatly in place with a braided leather headband. Within the

18

folds of his loose shirt were *shuriken* star blades and other fighting weapons. His bow and arrows, weapons unlike anything seen by the Apache, were resting inside the waiting stage. Ki considered practicing his deadly fighting skills but immediately rejected the idea, knowing it would attract too much attention.

Mr. Benjamin staggered out of a saloon across the street. Ki watched the man reach into his pockets and pull them inside out. With no money, he looked slightly desperate and very forlorn. He saw Ki watching him and he started to wave, then thought better of it and lowered his head to trudge down the street. Ki did not know if Mr. Benjamin had decided to go on to Yuma or not, but he hoped the pathetic creature decided to remain in this town. In a fight Mr. Benjamin would simply be one more person to worry about how to keep alive.

Ki joined Mrs. Wakefield and Jessie for a dinner of roast beef, a wilted salad, and apple pie. The hotel dining room was only half filled, and the conversation was sparse because even inside it was very warm. Dinner finished, Jessie insisted on paying for Agnes's meal.

"It'll be time to go soon," she said. "Perhaps we can even catch a few winks of sleep in the coach tonight if we don't take on many more passengers."

"That would be a blessing," Agnes said, "but not too likely for me. If they sent my husband off to Fort Yuma that suddenly, it means there's some pretty grave trouble along the road we'll be traveling across Arizona Territory."

Jessie excused herself and took Ki aside. "My concern is mounting," she said, slipping him a thick roll of greenbacks. "Before the general stores closes, I want you to buy a couple of extra rifles and plenty of ammunition. Also, buy some canteens and make sure that they are filled. If we are attacked, I think

19

our two shotgun guards are going to need all the help we can give them.''

Ki took the money. "Anything else?"

"Food for the event that we're attacked and the team is shot in its harness," Jessie said. "Buy some jerked beef and some tinned goods. Get anything else you can think of that would be helpful if we come under attack."

"I doubt I can find a cannon or a Gatling gun for sale," Ki told her.

"We could probably use both for insurance," Jessie said with a wry smile. "But Arizona is a big country, and I expect we'll slip through without interference."

Ki was not so confident. He took the money and left the Cattleman's Hotel and went down the boardwalk until he came to Putnam's General Store, where he'd dealt with the owner once or twice before.

Moses Putnam had been about to close his store, but now, with Ki's arrival, he quickly changed his mind. "How's Miss Starbuck?"

"She's fine," Ki said.

"This weather is a pistol, isn't it?"

"Sure is," Ki answered, walking over to the rifle rack and studying the weapons before he took a big old Sharps rifle in his hands. Guns and rifles were not his specialty, but sometimes you needed them in tight spots where a traditional samurai's weapons simply would not do. "Is this a good rifle?"

"Damn good. It's old and has seen a few rounds, but it's the most accurate weapon in the store. Single shot, though."

"Single but very long shot," Ki said. "How much?"

"For you, twenty dollars."

"I'll take it and two of these Winchester rifles along with about a hundred rounds of ammunition."

"You got 'em!"

"Oh," Ki said. "And one other thing."

"What's that?"

"Dynamite. Do you carry any?"

"Sure do, but do you mind telling me what you're planning to use it for?"

"I hope not to use it at all. I'm also going to need some beef jerky, three canteens, and some tinned goods."

"I hope Miss Starbuck brought some money."

"I brought the money," Ki said. "Load it up and I'll put it on the stage before the fresh horses are brought out."

"What's the matter? Don't you want the driver to see all this stuff?"

"That's right," Ki said. "I don't want to make him any more nervous than he already is."

"I'd be nervous, too, if I was going to Yuma. I need your business, but it'd be smart if you waited."

"That's what everyone is telling us," Ki said. "But we just can't."

"Your funeral if the Apache find you," Putnam said, shaking his head with disapproval.

As soon as the merchant had the goods sacked and Ki had paid his bill, the samurai hoisted the sacks over his shoulder and carried them across the street to the stagecoach. He carefully stowed everything inside and then closed the door and waited for the sun to go down.

When it did, he saw the driver come out and stare at the coach before shaking his head and turning to leave.

"Hey!" Ki shouted. "What's wrong?"

The driver was a tough-looking man with a knife scar down one side of his face. "My shotgun guards quit," he said. "They figure it's too dangerous to go on to Yuma."

Ki expelled a deep breath. "Where are they now?"

"Over at the Red Dog Saloon. Why?"

21

"Maybe I can get them to change their minds."

"Not a chance. I begged the bastards not to quit, but they wouldn't listen to me. Why should they listen to you?"

Ki pulled what was still a large roll of greenbacks from his pants and held the money up. "Because money speaks louder than words."

The driver chuckled. "Well, good luck! But if you're paying them a bonus to take you on to Yuma, I reckon as how I'm going to insist on equal pay."

"Sounds reasonable," the samurai said over his shoulder as he headed for the Red Dog Saloon.

It was a saloon just like a hundred others on the frontier, only maybe a little shabbier. It had a dirt floor and a big fly-specked print of Lola Montez, the famous "Spider Dancer," tacked to the wall. Behind a very scarred old bar hung a small mirror that had been busted and glued back together.

A few men were playing cards without much enthusiasm, and when Ki entered, he saw the two shotgun guards leaning against the bar with mugs of beer in their hands.

"You mind if I have a word with you men?"

The guards looked at the samurai. They knew who he was and both nodded. One of the guards, a man named Pete Bills, said, "I talk better when someone buys me a beer."

"So do I," his partner, Dean Reasons, said, finishing off his own beer and wiping the suds from his lips.

Ki ordered the pair fresh beers and ordered himself a sarsaparilla. He was not a drinking man. When their drinks were set up before them, Ki said, "My boss has to reach Yuma and so does Mrs. Wakefield. The driver says he won't go any farther without armed guards."

"Damn shame, that," said Pete with a sympathetic

22

cluck of his tongue. "So what do you want us to do about it?"

"I want you to change your minds."

"Why should we take the risk?"

Ki knew this was all a game, and he wasn't in the mood just now for games. "Because," he said, drawing the roll of money from his pants. "There's fifty dollars each for you to accompany us to Yuma."

"Not enough." Dean Reasons took a long pull on his beer. "You can't spend money with your scalp missing."

"All right, then, a hundred dollars, and if you don't accept, I'll find good men who will."

The pair exchanged questioning glances, and Pete nodded his head. "It's a deal. Let's see your money."

"Uh-uh," the samurai said. "You know that Miss Starbuck is good for it. It's payable when we reach Yuma. And by the way, bring your shotguns, but I've got a couple of extra Winchesters on board. Better weapons at longer range."

The two men grinned and it was Pete who said, "I tell you, it must be damn nice to work for a woman that is both rich and beautiful."

"It's not too bad," Ki said, reaching for his sarsaparilla, which he downed in one long draught. "Are you ready?"

The two guards finished their beers and followed the samurai out the door. The sun was just setting in the east and it was aflame. It seemed to scorch the mountains, and it made the Rio Grande appear to flow like liquid gold. If it had not been for the ovenlike heat and the dangers they faced, Ki would have stopped to admire the end of this day, but he had too much on his mind.

The driver was happy enough to work up a little jig. "Yah-hoo!" he cackled. "How much extra pay we getting, boys?"

23

"A hundred dollars when we reach Yuma," Reasons said.

"Well," the driver said, "if we *don't* reach Yuma, we sure won't have to worry about ever collecting our money!"

The driver thought it was good joke, but no one else did. Not Ki and certainly not the two sweaty guards. Fresh horses were brought out, and while the guards helped hitch up the team, Ki went to get Jessie and Mrs. Wakefield. He didn't know if he was happy or not that he'd gotten this venture back underway.

Only time—and the Apache—would tell.

★

Chapter 3

They rolled into a brilliant sundown as the stage swept across the hot, dusty country leaving a pillar of crimson dust to shimmer in the dying heat waves.

"Miss Starbuck, I want to apologize for my behavior this morning," Mr. Benjamin said. "I've been drinking pretty hard lately. Business hasn't been too good, and I've had a lot of personal tragedy in my lifetime."

Jessie looked at the drummer. "I think you owe Ki an apology, not me."

Benjamin swallowed. It was clear that he was going to have a difficult time apologizing to someone with almond-shaped eyes and a yellow cast to his skin, but to the man's credit he summed up the gumption to make his apology. "I was talking drunk and like a fool, Mr. Ki. I didn't even know what a samurai was until this morning."

"Forget it," Ki said without rancor.

"Thank you," Benjamin whispered, sitting up a little straighter. He still reeked of whiskey, but so far Jessie had not seen any indication that he had a bottle in his coat pocket. "I just miss my wife is all."

Mrs. Wakefield was too inquisitive not to take the bait. "Miss her? My good man, what happened to her?"

It was the question that the drummer had been hoping for. "They left me in Hannibal, Missouri," he said. "My wife was a farm girl, green as a gourd and mighty pretty when I first met her, if I do say so myself. Before life became so unkind, I was a pretty flashy kind of fella. Had nice clothes instead on these worn rags that you see me dressed in now. I had a wagon, a pretty team of sorrel mares, and I traveled around selling snake oil and liniments. All kinds of medicines and things like needles, threads, and even butter churns. Business was good."

"What changed it?" Mrs. Wakefield asked with impatience.

"Well," Mr. Benjamin said, leaning forward, hands on knees, "after the Missus and I got married, we traveled around for about a year before she decided she wanted to plant roots."

Benjamin's eyes rolled heavenward. "Can you imagine! Suddenly she got the idea that I should buy a farm!"

Jessie and Agnes exchanged curious glances. It did not seem like such a preposterous request for a woman to want to settle down and raise a family.

"I'm a professional man!" Benjamin cried with consternation written all over his face. "You should have heard me back in those days. I could sell a Bible to Satan himself!"

"I see," Agnes said. "So there was friction."

"You bet there was." Benjamin sighed deeply. "We both loved each other, honest to Pete we did.

26

But it got to the point that my dear Penelope became downright insistent about this farming business. Every time we spent the night at some farm, where for years my arrival had brought joy and excitement, she would start whining and moaning about what a wretched gypsy life she led. Pretty soon my very image was changed. From a dashing man of commerce, I came to be regarded as an insensitive clod.''

"Tsk, tsk,'' Agnes said, her eyebrows knitting with deep concern. "So what did you do?''

"I capitulated to her unreasonable request,'' the drummer said in a strangled voice that reflected all his bitterness. "Yes, I, Barnaby J. Benjamin, sold my medicine wagon and marshaled all my assets to buy a farm in Missouri. Sixty miserly acres of clods and rocks and weeds, two vicious mules, and a cabin unfit for human habitation.''

"Was your Penelope happy then?'' Jessie asked, herself captured by the story.

"Supremely so! She loved everything about that grubby little farm. Nary a complaint ever came from her lips as I toiled from sunup to sundown behind those . . . those awful, farting mules to raise a little corn, beans, and cotton.''

Ki's thin black mustache twitched as he struggled to keep from laughing out loud. Jessie dug her fingernails into her palms for the same reason and managed to keep a straight face and ask, "But the story turns tragic, doesn't it?''

"It had already become tragic! I became a stumbling, shambling wreck. I used a great deal of my first runty corn crop to make corn liquor. And after that I could not bear to face the mules again.''

"What were you feedin' those mules?'' Agnes asked.

Benjamin was caught off balance by the unexpected question and irritation flashed across his eyes.

27

"What can that possibly have to do with anything I've said?"

"Well," Agnes told him, "if you was feeding them mules green beans, of course they was farty! Now corn, or oats, that won't give 'em gas, but beans will every time."

Completely at a loss for words, Benjamin just stared at the woman in the twilight of their coach.

Jessie patted the man's sleeve. "What happened to your wife?"

"She met a California farmer," Benjamin confessed. "They ran off to the West Coast to grow alfalfa. My wife was very thrilled, but I'm sure that was worn off because the fellow was no good. Of course, I knew at once he was all talk."

"Of course," Agnes said. "Anyone who'd raise alfalfa in California couldn't possibly be trusted."

"That's right." Benjamin raised his chin. "She lives outside of San Diego. I'm on my way there to win her heart back, you may be sure. You see, Penelope doesn't realize it yet, but she loves me still, and I'm sure that she has long since realized her mistake and yearns for me to hold her in my arms again."

Jessie actually saw a tear slip from the shabby drummer's eye and roll down his cheek. The entire story was ridiculous, but there was not the slightest doubt in her mind that Barnaby J. Benjamin—a con artist to his whiskey-soaked core—was absolutely sincere in his quest to regain his Penelope.

"Why don't we try to get some sleep," Jessie said as the silence inside the coach stretched thin. "The next few days are going to be hard for all of us, and I'm sure that we need our wits about us."

Benjamin sighed again. "I am incapable of sleep since my Penelope has gone away. But I will seal my lips in pained silence until the dawn."

"Thanks," Jessie said. "What about you, Ki?"

"I will sleep for a while," the samurai told her without adding that, if there was Apache trouble in store for them, sleep would be helpful so that they all could be alert and best able to defend themselves.

Jessie had not really expected sleep to come as easily as it did, but when next she opened her eyes, the sun was rising behind them and the samurai was gone. She started for a moment and then realized that he would have climbed outside and taken a seat on the roof of the coach to watch the sunrise. He would probably be seated facing the sun and in a lotus position, and he would be meditating and thanking a higher power for all the wonders of this world. Even a world that had very little to offer except rock, sage, cactus, and dirt.

Ki was in fact enjoying the morning. The driver and the two guards had already lost interest in what they considered to be his very strange behavior. Now, seated cross-legged and with his arms loosely folded across his chest, the samurai's eyes were closed, and yet he was more aware of his immediate surroundings than anyone on board.

The bumpy road transmitted a million messages up through the rooftop and told him of its exact condition. The sun and the smells of sage told him the time of day and his position on the earth while his mind dwelled on the peacefulness of creating and the beauty there was in its great diversity.

"Hey, samurai!" the driver called. "If you go to sleep up here and fall off, you'll break your damn neck for sure. Better keep your eyes open."

Ki ignored the advice until Dean Reasons nudged his knee and said, "Wake up, dammit! If we got to sit up here in all this heat and dust and keep lookin' for Apache, then you ought to do the same."

Ki opened his eyes and regarded the men. "If Apache come, I will know of their arrival as soon as any of you."

"What are you gonna do, plug 'em with that crazy bow of yours?"

The three men chuckled, but Ki did not get angry. The presence of his unusually shaped samurai's bow always created a reaction because it was unlike anything seen on the American frontier. It was shaped so that, when fired, the bow itself would turn a half revolution of 180 degrees. Made of layers of glued wood wound at many points with red-colored silken thread, the bow's core was composed of two pieces of bamboo which gave an unusual amount of strength and flexibility. Ki could fire the bow almost as rapidly as a man could use a rifle, and he was phenomenally accurate with the weapon.

Pete Bills, the smaller of the two shotgun guards, said, "Me and Dean figure we should have gotten more money for this job. It's hell out here and we're sitting like targets for the Apache."

"You knew what you were buying into," Ki said.

"No, we didn't! But we learned at El Paso. You can't spend money if you're dead."

Ki closed his eyes. He had sensed for the last day or so that heat and fear were taking their toll on these men and that, little by little, they were talking their way out of going on to Yuma. Well, as far as the samurai was concerned, a deal was a deal. Ki expected the two guards and the driver to finish this trip to Yuma, and if they had other thoughts, there would be trouble.

It took them almost three days and most of three hot nights to finally reach Tucson to learn that the entire Arizona Territory was on an Apache alert. By then, the shotgun guards, worn down by the sun, the grit, and the beating they took up on the top as well as having their nerves stretched tight by the constant expectation of attack, were openly ready to quit.

"I don't reckon that a hundred dollars is worth

30

taking this damn coach the rest of the way to Yuma,"
Dean Reasons said as soon as they disembarked at
the Tucson stage depot. "Me and Pete been talking
it over. We got you halfway here; I think that means
you owe us half the money."

"No, it doesn't," the samurai said: "We had a
deal. You get paid in Yuma. Quit now and you get
nothing."

Reasons was the bigger of the pair and obviously
the leader. He stood at least six two and outweighed
Ki by a good thirty pounds of muscle. "Samurai,"
he warned, "we got a hundred dollars coming to the
pair of us and I reckon we earned ever red cent of it.
So pay up and there will be no trouble—for you, or
Miss Starbuck."

Ki stepped back and said in a very easy voice.
"There will be no trouble and I won't pay you. Not
until we reach Yuma."

Reasons knew that the samurai had overpowered
the young freighter and thrown him out of the speed-
ing coach somewhere east of El Paso. He wasn't
afraid of the smaller man, but he wasn't taking any
chances, either. "We don't want to hurt you."

"You won't."

Reasons scowled, then made his decision. He'd
crossed the line and several hostlers were watching,
and he wasn't about to look like a fool or a coward
in front of anyone. So he balled up his big fists and
hissed, "All right. If you gotta do this the hard way,
that's okay by me."

Reasons came in swinging, and Ki easily ducked
two roundhouse punches and launched a snap-kick
that caught the man in the groin and dropped him
white-faced in the dirt to gasp, "Git him, Pete!"

Pete was smarter. He simply went for his gun. But
before it was unholstered, cocked, and leveled to
fire, Ki's hand blurred downward and struck Pete's

31

wrist with a perfectly timed shuto-uchi or "knife-hand strike" that sent the revolver flying.

The speed and precision of Ki's attack completely unnerved the smaller man and he retreated, one hand clutching his injured wrist. "All right!" he said. "All right. You win! Keep the hundred dollars. You probably broke my damn wrist!"

Ki lowered his hands. "It's not broken, because I pulled up on the blow. You'd be no help against the Apache with a broken wrist," Ki said, looking at both men with little respect. "I'm not sure that either of you wil be much help anyway. But you're probably all I can get, so you'd better be on the stage when we leave in two hours."

Reasons had almost recovered from the kick to his crotch. "This is a free country, dammit! You can't make us take the stage to Yuma!"

"We have an agreement," Ki said. "And while nothing is on paper and it isn't legally binding, you've a moral commitment to helping both Miss Starbuck and Mrs. Wakefield live to see Yuma. I expect you to honor that commitment."

"And if we don't?"

"Then I'll come searching for you," Ki said, leaving it at that.

The two men looked damned worried when Ki left them, but he figured they'd be on the stage when it rolled on to Yuma. He wasn't sure that they'd be a whole hell of a lot of help to him, but something was better than nothing. Ki just hoped they could shoot better than they could use their fists.

A block down the street from the stage depot, Jessie entered the sheriff's office and found the sheriff fanning himself with a partially rolled-up newspaper. He was fiftyish, considerably overweight, and sweating in his stuffy little office. When he saw Jessie, however, he made a nice try at rolling his feet off his

32

desk and coming erect with a weak grin on his florid face.

"Afternoon, miss."

"Good afternoon," Jessie said, and introduced herself. "I am on my way to Yuma, and I would appreciate a little information."

"The only advice I'll give you is to stay here in Tucson until this Apache business is finished."

"That kind of advice is plentiful and probably very wise, but I and my friends are determined to continue westward. What I'd like to know is if you have had anyone murdered by strangulation in your town."

The sheriff sat down. He reached into his back pocket and pulled out a handkerchief and mopped his now grinning face. "We hung three greasers last week for horse thievin'. That's the same as stranglin' em, I believe."

Jessie was hot, tired, dirty, and in no mood for racial slurs or jokes. "If you hanged three Mexicans, I hope you did it for the same reason—and with the same amount of irrefutable evidence—that you'd need to hang three Anglos. But what I meant was, has anyone been murdered by strangulation within the last, say, two years."

"Sure! Next to gettin' shot or knifed, I'd say stranglin' was right up there with poison and beatin' people to death."

Jessie expelled a deep sigh of exasperation. "Let me be more specific. Has anyone in a prominent position been garroted? I am particularly interested in judges, prosecuting attorneys, and . . . well, I hate to say this, but sheriffs like yourself."

The man swallowed noisily and he dropped his pleasantness like a flea-infested coat. "Who are you, anyway? Some newspaper reporter or big-time magazine writer?"

"I'm a Texas cattle rancher," she said. "And that really has nothing to do with the question."

"All right," the sheriff said. "It's too darned hot to play pussyfoot with you, though most any man would want to. The fact is, we did lose Judge Hale about a year ago under those circumstances. He was found in his office strangled to death."

"And what about an investigation or even any clues leading to a suspect?"

"Oh, we hung the fella that did it. He was a drifter from Montana down on his luck. Judge Hale had sentenced him to a month in this jail for beating up a drunk and taking his money. This man got crazy mad and threatened the judge's life, and Judge Hale added another month to the sentence for good measure. The fella, his name was Ralph Larson, he just went crazy mad. I had to pistol-whip him and drag him off to jail."

Jessie leaned forward intently. "And then?"

"And then after he spent his time, he wasn't out of jail two days before he sneaked into the judge's office and strangled him with a rope or wire or something. He got away, but we found him in a saloon. Since there was no judge to pass sentence, I let the townspeople lynch the murderin' bastard."

"Did anyone actually see the murder committed? Or was there any real evidence?"

The sheriff looked pained. "Well, sure there was, miss! A whole courtroom of folks heard Ralph promise to kill the judge. What more evidence did we need to carry out justice?"

Jessie shook her head. "Why would this man strangle the judge—knowing full well he'd made a public threat on his life—and then be so stupid as to wait in some saloon for you to catch him?"

"Hell if I know. He swore up and down he was innocent. But they all do." The sheriff leaned forward, pulled out his handkerchief, and again mopped his sweaty face. "Say, what's this all about, anyway?"

"Did the judge leave any relatives? Any records? Anything that might have given you a clue to think that he was afraid of being strangled?"

"Nope. Judge Hale was tough and he was honest. In all the years I've been sheriff of this town, I never once saw him bat an eye at someone who threatened his life. He did what he had to do, same as me."

"What about relatives?"

"The judge left a widow."

"Is she still living here?"

"Sure. Where else would she live? The judge left her pretty well fixed. She's suffered plenty, but she's got a lot of sand in her craw. She lives over on Oracle Road just a few blocks from here. Second house east of Grant Road. Big two-story Victorian mansion. You can't miss it."

"Thank you," Jessie said. "You've been very helpful."

The sheriff frowned. "You ain't told me a darned thing. If there's something I should know, you better spit it out."

At the door Jessie turned and said, "Very well, I think it is entirely possible that you hanged the wrong man for the murder of Judge Hale. Good day, Sheriff."

Jessie found Ki, and together, they hurried over to Mrs. Hale's mansion and knocked on the widow's door. She was a strong-looking woman in her early sixties, tall with a great deal of presence. As soon as Jessie told her about the letter she had received at the Circle Star which had sent her rushing westward, Mrs. Hale immediately bid them to enter and showed them to her parlor. She rang for a Mexican maid, who brought them a delicious drink made of papaya and orange juice, with a slice of lemon to give it tang.

35

"I am so glad that someone has finally considered the possibility that my husband was murdered by a man other than Ralph Larson. I've said nothing of my doubts, but I've never been convinced that young Ralph was the real murderer."

"Why not?" Jessie asked.

"Because, he was simply a very desperate and drunk man himself the night he was first arrested."

"And the threats against your husband?"

"Empty threats. Ralph was a very intelligent young man. Only a fool would have carried out his threat and have remained to be arrested and lynched. And besides, I was so upset by the threats that I went to the jail and visited Ralph on a number of occasions. He was truly repentant."

"Do you have any idea who might have been the real culprit?"

"I would guess a cold-blooded killer named Joe Hagan. He was sent to the Yuma Penitentiary and served fifteen years. He escaped just two weeks before my husband's death, and he had threatened to kill Mr. Hale as recently as a month before his escape."

Jessie glanced at Ki. "Has the man been seen since his escape?"

"I don't know."

"Will you give us a detailed description of him?"

"Of course I will. Though you can get it from almost anyone."

"One final question," Jessie said. "Was anything taken during the commission of the murder?"

She nodded. "My husband had a beautiful gold ring with five diamonds embedded in it in this way."

Mrs. Hale drew a sketch of both the ring and Joe Hagan on a pad of paper and handed it to Jessie, who said, "You are quite an artist."

The judge's widow grew very tense. "If you find him and my husband's ring, kill the man and cut the ring from his finger—just as he did to my husband!"

Ki and Jessie exchanged glances, finished their drinks, and said their good-byes. Neither of them said another word about Joe Hagan that day.

Chapter 4

The vast Sonoran Desert lay sweltering under a thin veil of high, thin cloud which held the temperatures below 110 degrees but also made the days and nights unbearably humid. Inside the coach the passengers were suffering, especially Mrs. Wakefield. Benjamin's face remained flushed and he sweated profusely. Jessie had elected to climb up on the roof of the coach. There, at least, she could feel the whiff of an occasional breeze and study the harsh landscape that struggled on and on for hundreds of miles in every direction.

The only objects worthy of even a passing interest were the huge saguaro cactus with their fascinating shapes. Most were three- and four-armed, and some of the greatest ones reached forty and fifty feet into the air. The wickedly spiked staghorn cholla cactus were squatty, dangerous things that threatened any living creature that had the misfortune to brush their thorns. There were also barrel and ocotillo cactus and a sea of gray creosote bush.

In the daytime you saw nothing move except the clouds and an occasional hawk floating on the hot thermal winds that lifted from the scorched desert floor. But in the evening, and the early morning, the wildlife sought food and moisture. There were desert tortoises, huge and grimly determined to plod their way to whatever their destinations might be. Small mice were commonplace as well as almost comical jackrabbits with their giant ears. Now and then a roadrunner would burst across their dusty path, and the coyote was bold enough to watch the stage pass without fear so long as a gun or rifle was not pointed in its general direction.

All these things Jessie and Ki saw from the hot roof of the coach, but what they did not want to see were Indians, and so when a band of Apache suddenly appeared, a chill passed up and down their spines despite the temperature. The mounted Apache were about a mile up ahead, patiently waiting for the stage.

"Hand up them extra Winchesters and that big buffalo rifle!" Dean Reasons shouted down to the passengers below.

Ki said, "Jessie, you'd better get down inside. There looks to be at least thirty of them. Driver, slow the horses to a walk."

"Are you crazy!" Pete Bills shouted.

"No," Reasons said. "He's just being smart. Them Apache know we can't turn this damn thing around because of the soft sand. Hell, if I drive even three feet off this road, we'll sink to the axles and be easy pickings."

"We've come too damn far to turn around," the driver said, slowing his team to a walk. "When we get in rifle range, I'm going to give 'er hell, and everyone had better grab ahold tight."

Mrs. Wakefield and the drummer shoved the extra Winchester rifles as well as the Sharps out of the passenger windows where they were grabbed by outstretched hands.

"Dammit!" Reasons swore. "It looks like every last one of them has a Winchester, too!"

Ki slipped the sling of his quiver over his shoulder and took his bow in his fists. He selected "death song," a very special arrow with a small ceramic bulb fitted just behind the arrow head. The bulb had several precisely drilled holes, and when the arrow was unleashed, air passed through those holes and caused a high, screaming song that would fill even the bravest enemy's heart with great dread.

"Get a damn gun!" Reasons swore as the samurai nocked "death song" on his bowstring.

Jessie let the two guards take the Winchesters while she placed a cap on the percussion rifle and then spread out flat on the roof.

"That big gun will tear your shoulder off!" Pete warned.

"No, it won't," Jessie said between clenched teeth as she cocked the rifle and laid the barrel across the iron railing that normally served to hold the overflow luggage. "Just don't sent this team into a run until I fire."

The driver twisted around, started to say something in protest, then saw Jessie's grim face and the way she held the rifle. He closed his mouth and kept driving slowly toward the waiting Apache. "I count twenty-three," he said. "Oh, Lord, we are in for it now."

Jessie braced herself solidly and took aim. The moving coach made this a tricky shot, so she held her fire until she saw one of the Apache raise his rifle upward and then slam it down across the haunches of his thin pony. Jessie fired just as the pony bolted forward. The Apache in her sights disappeared for

40

an instant in a cloud of blue smoke that quickly dissipated to reveal a riderless horse leading the charge.

"Nice shooting!" one of the guards yelled.

"Hang on!" the driver shouted, his whip starting to pop as he drove the team into a hard run. "We sure as hell have come too damn far to turn back now!"

The Apache seemed taken by surprise that the coach did not swerve into the soft shoulder and attempt to turn around. And when the two shotgun guards opened fire and proved they could shoot better than they could fight, two more Indians were knocked from their ponies.

Ki stood up and drew the bow back until it bent nearly to breaking. When he released "death song," the arrow swept over the horses and soared to reach the lead rider. Even above the thundering of the coach and horses, the arrow's shriek could be heard, and the Apache charge faltered because of it. "Death song" seemed to hunt its victim like a missle, when it struck the Apache, the procelain bulb burst, and the song ended with a cry that lifted from its victim's throat.

The Apache broke to both sides of the road and rifles thundered as the stage swept past.

"They'll be coming after us!" the driver shouted.

Ki dropped to his knees and nocked another arrow just as a bullet struck Pete Bills and kicked him screaming off the stage. At almost the same moment, Agnes cried out in terror: "Mr. Benjamin! He's dead!"

"Get down on the floor!" Jessie cried to the woman. "Keep your head down!"

The horses were running full tilt, and the Indians had reversed direction and were coming after them. Looking over his head, the driver yelled, "This team won't run all the way to Yuma. We've got to find a place and make a stand!''

Ki saw a rocky hillock up ahead and yelled, ''We'll make our stand there!''

''I don't know if those horses can last that long at this speed!'' the driver shouted. ''Must be better than three miles.''

''Then ease them up a little,'' Jessie called, ''and we'll hold the Apache off with our fire!''

Jessie shoved the heavy Sharps rifle aside and Dean Reasons twisted around and opened fire. But now the Apache were out of firing range and seemed to be holding back.

''They know we'll kill the team if we try to outrun them,'' Ki said. ''The desert and time are both in their favor.''

''Look!'' Jessie shielded her eyes. ''They're splitting up and going off in two directions. They're trying to flank us and cut us off from those rocks!''

The driver's whip cracked again, and the heavily lathered team struggled forward in their harness as the coach surged ahead.

Jessie had a few moments and she used them to reload the Sharps. Dean Reasons reloaded his rifle, and Ki kept watching the distance between the rocks and the Indians who had easily drawn abreast of them and were now threatening to close in and deny them the rocky vantage point they would need to have any chance of making a defense.

''We ain't going to make it!'' the driver shouted. ''These horses are startin' to falter!''

''We've *got* to make it,'' Jessie said.

Somehow, the team of stage horses did manage to drag the coach slithering and skidding off the road and across the brush and cactus-strewn last few hundred yards. But it kept steady and deadly firing from the coach to bring off the feat.

The driver swung the coach in so close to the

boulders that it skidded and the left rear wheel struck a rock and shattered to splinters. The coach tilted far over and then collapsed in a heap with the team thrashing in their harnesses.

Jessie and Ki both threw themselves outward from the coach, and when Ki hit the ground, he rolled expertly and came up with his bow still in his fist. He nocked an arrow, and as the first Apache swept in with a shrill death cry, the samurai shot him through the heart.

Jessie tried to get her feet under her, but she was thrown so hard, that proved impossible. She struck the side of a rock and grunted with pain, then momentarily lost consciousness.

An Apache brave threw himself from his horse and raced forward, drawing his knife and reaching for Jessie's long, honey-blond hair. Ki drove the sharpened end of his bow into the warrior's belly, impaling him. Another warrior swept in and fired almost point-blank at the driver who was hurled over backward, mercifully dead before he struck a big clump of cholla cactus and quivered a moment before lying still.

"Aiii!" screamed more Apache as they swept in for the kill.

Jessie rolled sideways as bullets peppered the rock, and she grabbed her six-gun and fired almost blindly into the mass of attackers. Agnes pushed open the door of the overturned coach and tried to climb out, but a rider came sweeping in, and before the poor woman realized what was happening, the Apache slashed at her with the barrel of his rifle, and she fell unconscious back into the coach as the battle raged on.

The samurai dropped his bow and reached for his *tanto* knife with his left hand while his right dipped into his loose shirt and a *shuriken* star blade flashed brilliantly before it embedded itself in an Apache's forehead. Two more blades followed in lightning procession, as Dean Reasons took a bullet in the side but dropped to one knee, drew his gun, and emptied two more Apache saddles before the attack broke away and the Indians went racing off to regroup.

Jessie leapt to the coach and reached inside for the unconscious Mrs. Wakefield. The side of her face was covered with blood, and when Ki helped lift the poor woman out, she was barely alive.

"Let's put her in the shade of the rocks and out of sight of the Apache!" Jessie ordered.

As soon as Agnes was laid out, Jessie raced back to the coach, grabbed the canteens of water, and hauled them to the woman's side. She dashed water on Agnes's face and wiped the blood away, then raised her eyelids to study the woman's pupils. They looked normal enough, and Agnes's pulse was still beating steadily.

"You're going to live," she whispered to the unconscious woman. "We all are!"

The samurai tore the bloodied shirt off Dean Reasons and cut it into strips which he tied together and used to bind Reasons's wound. "Are you going to be able to shoot straight?"

Reasons nodded. "It doesn't look like I have much choice. Uh-oh, here they come again!"

Jessie snatched up a rifle and opened fire as the Indians came racing in at them. The air shook with the roar and thunder of rifle fire, and the Apache took a shocking toll as their attack failed and many riderless horses went bounding off through the sage.

"They won't do that again," Ki said. "They've taken too many losses already."

"How can you be sure?" Reasons demanded, wiping his sweat from his eyes and grimacing with pain.

"I've fought them before," Ki said. "They've no more interest in dying than we have."

44

"So what will they do?"

"They'll do absolutely nothing." Ki glanced up at the sun that was breaking through the clouds. "They'll figure we can't stay here in this heat more than a day or two. They know that you're wounded. They'll figure we might have a canteen or two, but no more and perhaps not even any food and that we're low on ammunition."

Jessie scooted over beside the wounded guard. "Let me see the wound," she said. "If we're going to be caught up in a waiting game, it's got to be attended to."

The samurai said, "The bullet is still inside of him. Probably lodged in between his bottom ribs."

"It'll have to come out or the wound will become infected."

But Dean Reasons shook his head. "Miss Starbuck," he said, "right at this minute I'm still alive and that's plenty good enough. If you try and dig the bullet out, you might cut a big one, and I'll bleed to death for sure."

"There are no arteries or veins in that area."

"Oh, yeah! Well why the hell am I bleeding like a stuck pig?"

"I don't know the answer to that," Jessie admitted. "But I've dug out a lot of bullets and no one has died from it yet."

"I don't aim to be the first," Reasons swore, hugging the sopping bandage to his side. "Besides, if the Apache decide they don't want to wait like your samurai friend says, then you'll need my gun in a hurry. Hell, what good would I be then?"

Jessie looked up at the samurai. "If I don't dig that bullet out," she said to Ki, "he's as good as dead right now."

The samurai understood what she was asking him to do, and his hand moved quickly to the *atemi* or pressure point near the base of Reasons's thick neck.

45

Driving his thumb down into the flesh, Jessie saw a flicker of protest rise up in the man's eyes but die as blood was instantly cut off from his brain and he lapsed into a state of unconsciousness.

"I don't know how you can do that so quickly," she said. "I've tried it a time or two, and I can't get it to work at all."

"It takes a lot of practice," the samurai admitted. "Shall I start a small fire?"

Jessie looked over the rocks at the Apache who had dismounted and were mostly hidden in the brush. "Might as well. We sure aren't going to hide anything from them. How many are left?"

"I'd say at least ten," the samurai replied. He used his blade to cut through tough branches of sage until he had a small pile and started a fire. The sage burned rapidly, which was fine with Jessie. She placed a half-empty canteen in the fire after uncapping the lid. Within five minutes the canteen was boiling, and the samurai used two flat rocks to lift it out of the coals.

"Remove the bandages," Jessie said, keeping one eye on the Apache.

The samurai removed the bandages and handed Jessie another clean strip of cloth, which she carefully dampened and then used to sponge away the already caked blood so that she could see the seeping bullet hole.

"It's a good thing that he was hit with a bullet rather than an arrowhead," Ki said. "It would have done a lot more damage."

"That's true, but it would have been easier to get out. Help me roll him over a little."

Jessie studied the bullet hole and tried to calculate the angle of entry and thus judge where the bullet would be found. "I think I had better go in from the front," she said.

Ki unsheathed his knife, passed it twice through

46

the flames and then gave it to Jessie. "I'll give him another touch," the samurai said, applying *atemi* once more to be sure that Reasons was not going to come awake thrashing about in pain.

Jessie drew a deep breath and slipped the narrow but very sharp blade into the bullet hole. Sweat beaded on her forehead and ran down to sting her eyes, but she did not bother to wipe it away. "I don't feel anything hard and loose," she said after almost a full minute of delicate probing.

The samurai mopped her forehead. "Like you said, if it isn't found and removed, he's a dead man."

"Roll him over again," Jessie ordered. When Reasons's back was turned to her, she palpated the flesh in some desperate hope that she might feel a hard mound indicating the presence of a bullet just under the surface. But when it was clear that no such indication was forthcoming, Jessie pressed the blade of the knife down at the point where she guessed the bullet should have exited and then cut into the muscle.

She closed her eyes, all her concentration focusing on her fingers. "There," she whispered, "it's right between the ribs as you said it would be. I'm going to have to cut him a little more to get it out."

"It's just muscle," the samurai said. "Don't think, just do what has to be done."

Jessie made the incision wide enough to insert her index finger, which she slid down alongside the blade until she could roll the lead bullet up and out of the wound. She stared at the bloody and smalled ball for a minute before tossing it away from her. "It's always amazed me how such a tiny piece of lead can kill a big man—sooner or later."

Jessie had not brought along a needle or thread, so she just bound both the entry and her own exit wound up as tight as possible and prayed that Dean Reasons would not become infected inside and that he would regain consciousness in time if another attack came from the Apache.

Having done all she could with the man, Jessie went back and saw to Agnes, who was just beginning to regain consciousness. The woman's eyes fluttered and she stared up at Jessie. "What happened?" she breathed.

Jessie told her, not bothering to add the fact that only she and Ki were fit enough to fight if the Apache attacked.

"Have we got any chance at all?"

"Of course!" Jessie forced a smile. "When the stage doesn't show up in Yuma, the Army will come to our rescue, and I'll bet your own husband will be riding out in front."

"He will be," Agnes said hopefully. "If the telegraph lines haven't been cut, then Yuma will know we're in trouble. But what about the Indians?"

"They've taken pretty heavy losses themselves," Jessie said. "I think they'd like to wait us out a few days and see if we don't try and run for it. This Arizona sun can do strange things to people. It can make them act foolishly."

Agnes agreed. "It can boil your brains and we'll need water. Lots of water."

"We have it," Jessie said. "At least four canteens full."

She looked to the samurai. "You'd better go over there and cut the horses free. We don't have enough water to keep them alive and they'll die for sure if left in their harness."

"If I cut them loose, the Apache will just catch and eat them," Ki said. "Unless . . ."

"Unless what?"

"Unless I can get to their own ponies tonight and drive them off."

"Can you?"

Ki nodded his chin up and down. "If I can do

48

that, and also manage to kill a few more, we just might convince them that this is a waiting game they are sure to lose.''

Jessie glanced up at the sky. There was still about two hours until dark, and the coach horses were already suffering. Reasons had shot one which obviously had a busted leg, and another had been killed by a stray bullet. But two were still alive, lying on their sides all tangled up in their harness.

''All right,'' she said. ''Go ahead and try after the stars come out. With any luck, there will still be enough overhead clouds to block out most of the moonlight.''

Ki agreed. It was not his nature to sit and wait when he could take destiny into his own hands. And besides, in his bag, still resting inside the overturned coach, was his black ninja costume. Tonight, when he became ninja, he would teach the Apache what it meant to face an invisible assassin. And those that lived to see tomorrow's sunrise might even decide that it was *they* who had somehow become the hunted.

Chapter 5

The Apache built a huge fire that night and danced until long after midnight, mourning the loss of their tribesmen and vowing to make the survivors of the stagecoach suffer unimaginable pain before they were killed. Their cries and laments filled the desert air, and several times mournful coyotes joined in with their own sad chorus.

But at last the Apache fire died low, and the warriors, having slaughtered one of their own ponies and gorged on its stringy meat, lay down and fell into a deep slumber. By that time the samurai was almost in their midst. Dressed in a black ninja costume complete with a hood so that only his eyes were visible, Ki appeared almost ethereal. In Japan he had spent thousands of hours learning how to slip undetected among his enemies. The old *rōnin* had taught him to blend in with his surroundings, to move like a tiger in the forest which stalked its unwary prey without being seen or heard until its powerful fangs and claws were buried in flesh.

Ki materialized as if out of nowhere, and when he stood beside the smoky Apache camp, he silently counted ten Apache sleeping on the ground. There was no guard on watch because it never occurred to these brave and cunning warriors that their camp would not be safe from attack.

First, Ki thought, the ponies. He moved swiftly toward the picket line, and when a small dun saw him, its head shot up and it stomped the ground nervously, but the ninja whispered, "Do not be afraid, little horse. If I turn you lose, you will not be eaten like your brother."

Ki's voice was soothing and the dun quieted. The ninja touched its soft muzzle, then his other hand drew his *tanto* blade across the picket line so that it severed as easily as if he had drawn a hot blade through warm butter. Ki moved to the next pony and the next, his blade slicing each picket rope. One by one, the ponies drifted off into the sage. Once they had probably belonged to either Mexicans or whites along the border, and Ki was reasonably certain that was where they would be heading now.

With the ponies gone, Ki turned his attention back to the Apache camp. He moved into it and stood among the sleeping warriors with his hand resting on the handle of his knife. It would be very easy to simply slit the throats of his enemies, and the ninja knew full well that they would not have hesitated to do the very same thing to him. Ki pulled out his knife and stood beside one sleeping warrior. The firelight revealed an Indian in his late teens, a boy, really.

The samurai knelt down beside the sleeping warrior and studied his face. In sleep, the Apache looked very innocent, but in life . . .

Ki stood up and then, without really thinking

51

about it, he walked over to an Apache and took his rifle up and began to empty it into the campfire. At the first shot the Apache were jumping to their feet in wild confusion, and at the second and third shots, with sparks and embers showering into the air, the confusion became chaos.

The first warrior who seemed to understand that an enemy was right among them tried to scream a warning as he jumped at Ki, but the samurai shot him and danced lightly aside before he clubbed another Apache and then leapt through the campfire, shrieking his own victory cry before he vanished into the darkness.

Most Apache were superstitious, and those who had seen Ki believed that some kind of demon had passed through their camp. One Apache who thought differently ran out of his protective circle of firelight and died with a *shuriken* blade embedded in his forehead.

Ki, moving soundlessly and like a dark shadow, seemed to glide across the desert until he returned again to the rocks where Jessie, Agnes, and the now conscious Dean Reasons were waiting.

Ki leaped in among his friends, only slightly out of breath from his exertions, as the disraught cries of the Apache filled his ears.

"My God!" Agnes Wakefield breathed. "What kind of a man are you!"

Ki said nothing but Jessie was quick to his defense. "He's a samurai, and tonight he was also ninja. The Apache are cunning and there are no more dangerous men in this kind of land, but they do not possess the skills of a ninja."

"A what?" Reasons asked in a voice made weak from the loss of blood.

Jessie did not answer. "How many are left?"

"Eight," the samurai replied. "Just eight."

"Do you think they will still attack in the morning?"

"I don't know," Ki said honestly. "My guess would be that they will decide this is an evil place and that the spirits are against them here."

"Even if they go, how are we going to reach Yuma?" Agnes whispered, still not able to take her eyes off of Ki dressed in his hooded ninja outfit.

"The two stagecoach horses are still alive," Jessie said. "And while you were gone, I cut them free of their harness and got them into these rocks."

"Do they seem sound?"

"Yes," Jessie said. "They're big, strong animals, and if we give them just two canteens of our water, they might be able to carry all of us out of here."

Ki nodded. "I ran the Apache's ponies away. But if they decide to come after us on foot, they'll easily overtake us. You know how they can travel in this country."

"I know," Jessie said. "But we either attempt to reach Yuma, or we stay here and hope that help arrives before more Apache. I think we should make a run for it."

"Hell yes, we should!" Reasons said. "This country is crawling with Indians. The longer we're out here, the slimmer our chances to get away clean."

"I've already asked them if they're strong enough to ride," Jessie said. "They both agree that they are."

"Then let's go now," Ki said, grabbing up his bow and the canteens. "We still have a good five hours before daylight. The road is clear, and if I've driven terror and confusion into the Apache camp, we ought to have a pretty good head start before morning when they decide that the spirits might be more favorable down the road a ways."

So, the decision to run was made and the two surviving coach horses were brought out of the rocks.

"What if they've never been ridden?" Reasons asked.

"They have," Jessie said. "I've already mounted both to make sure. Come on, Agnes, we'll help you up behind Ki."

The samurai jumped lightly up on the near horse, and with Jessie's help, Agnes Wakefield was able to climb a rock and ease herself down behind the samurai. Jessie mounted the second horse, and Reasons, his face white with pain, mounted with some difficulty behind her.

"Let's ride," Jessie said, "but try to keep the rocks between us and the Apache camp for a few miles before we angle back to the stage road. With a little luck, they won't even know that we've gone until tomorrow morning."

They rode around the pile of rocks and then headed northwest. The two big coach horses were rough-gaited, and without saddles it was a misery trying to dodge cactus and avoid deep, dry arroyos. Agnes suffered whenever her horse faltered and took a particularly rough step, while Jessie could hear the man behind her take a sharp intake of breath.

Sunrise was spectacular. It came up and almost at once the air grew very warm. Agnes clutched the samurai while behind her, Reasons held Jessie with a steadily weakening grip. Sometime just before mid-morning, he rolled sideways and toppled to earth. Fortunately, he missed cactus.

"I'm finished," he whispered when Ki and Jessie rolled him over. "Put a bullet through my skull and ride on without me. It's your only chance."

Jessie stood up and studied their backtrail. She couldn't see any sign of the Apache, but that meant nothing. Besides, now they were afoot and even more dangerous. An Apache could cover a hundred miles of searing desert in less than twenty-four hours. He could move across country that would defy a horseman and require a fraction of the water.

"What do you want to do?" Ki asked.

Jessie frowned. "Let's ease him up on the horse and try to get back to the road. The only thing we can do is to keep moving and hope to stay one step ahead of the Apache."

"I could stay here," Ki said. "I could wait for them and maybe . . ."

"No," Jessie said quickly. "Last night you were ninja. You caught them by surprise and drove fear and confusion into their minds. But today, out here in this white-hot country, they'd know you—not as some dark demon—but as a man. You cannot stand up against all of them. They'll kill you."

"But not before you and Mrs. Wakefield were many miles closer to Yuma."

"No," Jessie said. "We stay together. If Reasons can't go much farther, then we search for a place to make our stand."

"After giving the horses the water that they needed to get this far, we have precious little for ourselves," Ki reminded her. "I think I need to stay behind."

"No," Jessie said firmly. "We have been in worse spots than this, and we've always managed to pull through."

"I will do as you wish, but . . ."

Jessie placed her hand on the samurai's shoulder. "Change out of your ninja costume and prepare to come with us."

Ki turned away from Jessie. He could not and would not defy her unless the very moment arrived when the choice between her life and his own could not be postponed. At that point he would stay behind no matter what she said.

By late afternoon Ki knew that the Apache had regrouped and were on their backtrail. He had seen them cross over a low raise of ground, and they were less than ten miles back and coming at the same

55

tireless trot that he himself had often used to cover long distances on foot.

Dean Reasons had lost consciousness hours ago, and they had tied him across the broad back of Jessie's horse. It was an arrangement that would do at a walk, but a trot or a gallop would kill the man for sure. Besides that, Agnes Wakefield was so weak that she could barely hang on to Ki. For her also, trotting or galloping was out of the question.

As evening approached and the Apache grew larger and larger on their backtrail, Jessie and Ki knew that a decision had to be made.

It was Ki who had the answer. "We can't outrun them and we can't expect help to suddenly arrive," he said.

"So where does that leave us?"

"With the dynamite I bought with the money you gave me in El Paso," he said, patting his bag.

Jessie's eyebrows shot up. "You never told me about dynamite!"

"I forgot about it until after I raided their camp last night. If I'd have tossed a few sticks into their campfire, none of this would have happened to us today."

"Where is it!"

"In that big shoulder pack that I slung over this horse's neck," the samurai said almost cheerfully. "It sort of changes the complexion of things, doesn't it."

Jessie almost laughed. "I can't believe it!"

"And I can't believe I forgot about it last night."

Jessie pulled her horse to a halt. "So how do you propose we use it?"

"I haven't thought that far," Ki admitted. "Dynamite is not exactly the weapon of choice for a samurai. And because the Apache following us have rifles, we are sure not going to be able to just toss it into their midst."

Jessie frowned. "Ki," she said, "it's darned unlikely that they'll sleep tonight so that you can slip
into their camp again. So I guess that means we'll
have to let them come to us. We've got to find a trap
to set for them, and we've got to do it fast."

"How about that crest of land out there?" he said,
pointing to a low, rocky hillock.

"What is your idea?"

Ki shrugged his shoulders. "My idea is that we
just disappear over the top and wait on the other side
for them to get within pitching range."

Jessie frowned. "That's not a very sophisticated
plan, Ki."

"Out here, simple works best."

Jessie understood what he was saying. And as
often as not, simplicity did win the day. "All right,
but let's slow it down a little. I want them to be
close behind us when we top that hill and light those
fuses."

They left the stage road and angled hard across the
desert. The horses were stumbling with exhaustion
and gaunt for lack of food and water. It hurt and
worried Jessie to see that, despite the searing heat,
they were so dehydrated they were not even sweating. Unless they found water, Jessie knew they would
not last another twelve hours.

It seemed to take forever for them to top the ridge,
and the Apache, spread out in a skirmish line, were
running as if they could go on and on without ever
faltering.

Ki jumped from his horse as soon as they were out
of sight of the Indians, and he pulled Agnes down
with him and laid her on the sand, in the shade of a
tall saguaro. Reasons slipped off Jessie's horse and
collapsed like a rag doll.

"Here," Ki said, handing Jessie two sticks of
dynamite and taking two for himself. "I think this
will discourage our friends."

The samurai led Jessie back up almost to the crest of the ridge. "Stay down until I say so and then light both sticks and throw hard and far."

Jessie trusted her ability with a gun, but she had serious reservations about her ability to use dynamite. Besides, there were other questions. "How will you know when to throw them?"

"We'll both hear them. These Apache aren't trying to be silent. All they want is to get into rifle range before darkness falls. They'll be coming very fast, and we'll hear their movement."

They waited no more than five minutes, and with poor unconscious Agnes and Dean Reasons stretched out in the brush, Jessie knew that there was no room for error. If the dynamite failed or if . . . hell, she thought, why even think about it? Her six-gun was resting on her shapely hip, and besides the dynamite, Ki had more deadly *shuriken* blades. If they had to make a stand, this would be as good a place as any.

"Here they come!" the samurai whispered as he struck two matches and gave her one. "All right, light them both!"

Jessie's fingers were shaking as she lit the fuses and held the two sticks at arm's length. She watched the fizzling fuses burn down to within an inch of the dynamite with mounting fear until the samurai said, "Now!"

Ki jumped up and hurled both sticks, and Jessie's went flying only a few seconds later. She could not even see the Apache that would be scaling the other side of the ridge, but when the four blasts went off, the entire ridge seemed to buckle and rock. A tremendous shower of dirt, rock, and even a hug saguaro cactus exploded high into the air and then rained down on them. Ki threw his body across Jessie's and protected her from harm.

The debris rained down on them for a good fifteen seconds, and the two stage horses were so frightened that they did not stop running for almost a mile. But Jessie and Ki hardly noticed as he edged over the ridge and peered down the devastated slope.

"Where did they go?" she whispered.

The samurai's brown eyes rolled heavenward and Jessie's green eyes followed.

"All of them?"

"It would appear so," Ki told her. "All gone to the happy hunting ground."

"Wow," Jessie whispered. "At least they all went together and in a great blaze of glory."

Ki went and caught the horses and brought them back. The huge explosion had made them both spooky, but they were so desperately thirsty that they seemed to understand their only hope was in sticking with humans. They stood patiently while Jessie and Ki pushed Agnes and Reasons up and over their broad backs.

"Let's tie them down and walk back to the road. Maybe we'll find water before tomorrow morning."

Ki shook the canteens. "We've still one full one and another half full."

"In this country that won't take us too far," Jessie said. "And if we haven't found more water by morning, I'll be forced to shoot these poor suffering animals before I'd make them face another day. I'd do that right now if it wasn't that they are so desperately needed to carry Agnes and Dean."

Ki was not the horseman that Jessie was, but he figured the horses would be dead by sunrise if they didn't drink. And one thing was certain, they could not spare a drop of water for animals.

The night passed much as a long nightmare passes. Jessie was so tired and thirsty that she could not swallow. On two occasions they stopped, unloaded Agnes and Reasons, then poured life-giving water down their gullets. Fortunately, the pair held the water even when they were hoisted across the animal's backs.

At daybreak Jessie and Ki stopped and stood swaying with fatigue. "Is it a mirage?" Ki asked.

"I don't think so," Jessie said, her voice sounding like two pieces of sandpaper being rubbed together. "I think it is the United States Army."

Jessie's eyes filled with tears, which surprised her because she didn't think she had a drop of water left in her body to spare. But the tears were real and when the sweet, lovely sound of an army bugle split the air, Jessie sagged to her knees and said her prayerful thanks.

Chapter 6

Yuma, resting at the junction of the Colorado and Gila rivers, was almost in a state of siege when they arrived because its citizens well remembered that Yuma had a bloody history. In 1781 the Indians had massacred her inhabitants, and there had been a great deal of warfare ever since. Named after the Yuma Indians discovered by the Spaniards in 1540, the town had eventually become a mission settlement as trade between California soon created steamship navigation companies ferrying goods and troops from ports as far away as San Francisco. For a time, Yuma had been known as Arizona City, but now the territorial prison had been built, and it was rumored that the Southern Pacific Railroad was soon to be started and would link Yuma with El Paso.

One of Jessie's first duties upon her arrival was to get Agnes and Dean Reasons to a doctor, and they were told that the army post surgeon was exceptional. Also, soon after their escort into Fort Yuma, Jessie had the pleasure of witnessing the tearful reunion of Mr. and Mrs. Wakefield. Agnes was battered and suffering from heat exhaustion. Her eyes had blackened from the Apache blow to her head, but she was alive and Jessie had no doubt that she'd soon be fully recovered.

Sergeant Wakefield, a tall, stern-looking man with close-cropped gray hair and a square chin, approached Jessie and Ki to say, "You saved her life and I want you to know that I'll always be in your debt."

"Your wife is very courageous," Jessie said. "She was warned to stay in El Paso, but she had to come and be at your side. You can be proud of her."

The sergeant's gruff demeanor softened. "Agnes is a soldier, same as me. But she says that you and this . . . what'd you call him?"

"I'm a samurai," Ki said, looking up at the powerful career soldier.

"Yeah," Wakefield said. "Well, she said that you're meaner than a passel of pissed-off polecats. She said you dress funny and shoot a backward bow and throw little star blades. Me, I take that with a grain of salt, figuring the sun fried her brain a little out there. But no matter, I owe you both her life, and if there's ever any trouble you can't handle, give me a holler and I'll come runnin' no matter where I am or what the consequences. You understand what I'm sayin'?"

"I do," Ki said, somehow feeling more threatened than complimented.

Jessie felt a hand on her arm, and she turned to see the young army doctor. "I wanted to talk to you in private for a minute," he said. "My name is Lieutenant Jason Caldwell."

He was a bronzed six-footer with sandy hair and intelligent, pale blue eyes. Jessie allowed him to lead her up to the porch of the post dispensary. "Is something wrong?"

"No," he said, studying her intently. "Everything is suddenly very right."

Their eyes measured each other with more than a casual interest.

"Then what did you want to discuss?"

He finally managed to tear his eyes off of her, glance to the side, and then say, "I wanted to know where you learned to do such skillful surgery with a sheath knife."

"I've taken a few bullets out of men," she told him. "I've also known a few surgeons like yourself and have availed myself of their knowledge."

"I'm not a surgeon," he said quickly. "I'm just an overworked and underpaid army doctor."

"I'm sure you've done a lot of surgery, no matter how brief your career has been thus far." Jessie sighed. "With all the talk of the Apache raids, I'm afraid that you might have to do a great deal more."

His smile evaporated. "Yes," he said quietly, "I know what you mean. But these Apache uprisings have a history of quieting down just as fast as they spring up. First we had Cochise, now Geronimo, and there are at least three or four other Apache leaders always raiding along the Mexican-American border. They're as elusive as smoke."

"Will Mr. Reasons live?"

"Yes," the doctor said. "He's lost far too much blood, but if he rests, he'll be back to normal in a few months. Your Japanese bodyguard also took quite a bit of punishment himself. In fact, you're the only one of the survivors of that ill-fated stagecoach run that seems to have fared well."

"I shouldn't have insisted on coming here to Yuma no matter what the costs," Jessie said. "But my mission was urgent."

"Is there any way I can help you on your mission?"

63

Jessie smiled. "It's a small town; would you know a Mrs. Cassandra Hastings?"

The doctor blinked. "Why, of course! Everyone in Yuma knew her late husband, Judge Hastings. His death was a tragedy of major proportions. We still haven't gotten a replacement. And as for Mrs. Hastings, well, she is a lovely woman. A jewel in a patch of thorns."

Jessie thought that an odd way to put it, but decided to say nothing. "I need to see her at once."

"Are you friends?"

"No," she replied, "we've never met, but I was a very close friend of her husband."

"Let me escort you to her home," the doctor said.

"Shouldn't you be here in case of some emergency?"

The doctor chuckled. "Believe me, Mrs. Starbuck, Yuma is not so large that they can't find me almost at a moment's notice."

Jessie realized how true that statement was. Yuma was not a quarter as large as El Paso, and if it had not been for the territorial prison and the fort, Yuma would have been little more than a riverside village. "All right," Jessie said, "I accept your offer."

"I think I'll find us rooms at the hotel," Ki said.

"There are only three hotels, and the only one that Miss Starbuck would find suitable would be the Horizon Hotel," the doctor said. "And I can see that she finds her way there."

Ki looked at Jessie and when she nodded that it was all right, he walked away.

"So," the doctor said as they walked up a tree-lined residential street. "What do you do for a living, Miss Starbuck?"

Jessie looked up at him. "I ranch down in Texas. Run some cattle."

"How many?"

"About fifteen thousand."

Dr. Jason Caldwell stopped dead in his tracks. "Did you say fifteen thousand head of cattle?"

She nodded. "Give or take a thousand."

"Holy mackerel! That is a lot of beef! How'd you come by so many?"

"It's a big country and there were a lot of long-horns running loose after the Civil War. My father, along with men like Goodnight and Richard King, saw an opportunity. I've sort of expanded the Circle Star Ranch since my father's death, and it's the life I've chosen to lead when I'm not traveling on business."

Caldwell shook his head. "It appears that I'm totally out of my league with you, Miss Starbuck. I'd been thinking I might boldly invite you to accompany me to dinner, but I'm beginning to see that there is nothing I could offer a woman of your means that would come close to being impressive."

Jessie was amused. She saw no point in agreeing that Yuma had little to offer a world traveler but, on the other hand, the doctor was obviously a handsome young man who might be able to tell her a great deal about the death of Warren Hastings. He might even be able to shed some additional light on the true identity of the Arizona Strangler.

"I would enjoy your company for dinner," Jessie said as they approached the elegant, two-storied home of Cassandra Hastings. "Please come by the Horizon Hotel for me at eight."

"Don't you want me to introduce you to Mrs. Hastings?"

"No," Jessie said, "that won't be necessary. She's the one that sent an urgent message asking me to come to Yuma, and I'm sure we will acquaint ourselves without any problems."

The young doctor looked a little disappointed, and Jessie wondered if he also had thought of asking the widow Hastings out to dinner after a proper period of mourning.

"All right," he said. "Eight o'clock for dinner."

"Eight o'clock," she repeated, giving him a winning smile. "In the lobby of the hotel."

He tipped his hat, beamed, and said, "Right!"

Jessie watched him stride back toward the fort, and she thought he was probably a very good man. He actually reminded her a little of poor Warren Hastings, with the boyish way he smiled and his confident stride.

Jessie knocked on the door, and it was opened by a woman that could be none other than Mrs. Hastings. She was quite beautiful, with long black hair and large, exotic eyes. Her skin was as white as alabaster and absolutely flawless. When she spoke, her voice had a slight huskiness to it that Jessie imagined would attract men in droves. She was shorter than Jessie, but equally well endowed, and dressed in the black of mourning, she made an arresting figure. One that would turn the heads of men on any capital street in the world.

"Mrs. Hastings, my name is Miss Jessica Starbuck."

Cassandra Hastings's reaction was instantaneous. She threw her arms around Jessie and hugged her with all of her might. "How glad I am to see you come at last!"

Jessie finally pulled free. Holding the woman at arm's length, she saw that Cassandra's eyes were misted with tears. Jessie touched the young woman's cheek. "I am so sorry about your late husband," she said. "Warren was one of the finest men I ever knew."

"He admired you greatly," Cassandra replied, "and it's easy to see why. You are a stunning-looking woman. One I am told has more than enough brains and courage to match your beauty."

66

"I came as soon as I could. We had some trouble, but that is past now."

Cassandra closed the door behind her and said, "Come have some tea with me. We have so much to discuss."

Jessie followed the woman into her kitchen when Cassandra made the tea. She placed it in a teapot and added sugar and then put everything on a silver tray which she carried into the parlor.

"So many books," Jessie said, admiring three floor to ceiling bookcases.

"Yes, but I admit that most of them were enjoyed by my late husband. Warren was an inveterate reader. When relaxing, you almost never saw him without a book."

They sat down and Cassandra poured the tea, and when they had talked for several moments about the hot weather and the Apache, the woman said, "I probably had no right to send that rather hysterical note. Perhaps I panicked and you needn't have come to Yuma at all."

"Please let me be the judge of that," Jessie said. "Besides, it's my understanding that you had not seen the letter that your husband wrote and sealed, is that true?"

"It is," she said.

Jessie produced Warren Hastings's letter, and when his widow had finished reading it, she was pale. Her hands were shaking so badly that when she tried to sip her tea, she wound up spilling it into its saucer. Setting the cup down with a nervous rattling sound, she managed to whisper, "So, he knew that he was targeted by someone he called the Arizona Strangler."

"It would appear so," Jessie said. "He had obviously spent a great deal of time researching the man's background in a vain attempt to discover his identity."

"He never mentioned a word about a crude drawing of a man hanging by a noose being drawn on his office door," Cassandra said, covering her face with her hands for a moment as she struggled to retain her composure. "My God! If only he'd given me some indication! I would have insisted that we leave Arizona Territory at once!"

"He wouldn't have run," Jessie said. "You know that better than I do. Warren was a lawman. A crusader for justice and an unwavering champion of the law. No, he'd have stayed."

Jessie placed her cup and saucer down on the hearth and walked over to kneel beside the shaken woman. "Your husband said he had compiled a list of suspects and placed it in his safe. I need to find that list."

"Yes," Cassandra breathed. "Of course. If we don't find out who killed him and the others that he wrote about, then it could go on and on."

Cassandra Hastings had to visibly get a firm hold on herself, and Jessie appreciated the control that she exercised. It took a very strong woman to face the fact that her husband had died at the hands of a "diabolical beast," as he had described the killer. It also took a strong woman to remain in Yuma when all indications were that her own life might be in serious jeopardy.

"I'll open the safe," Cassandra said, after a long moment in which she pulled herself together.

"Thank you."

Jessie followed the widow into her husband's study. Although the windows were all tightly sealed and the room had obviously been closed up since her husband's murder, there was already a film of dust on the furniture and the polished hardwood floors. As in the parlor, the room was walled by bookshelves, but in here they were mostly scholarly tomes. Jessie saw row after row of titles that pertained to the law. Warren Hastings had possessed a very orderly and scholarly mind. He should have been a professor of law and could have been but had instead chosen to practice his profession on the frontier where it was most needed. Considering his intellect, courage, and dedication, it was small wonder that Warren had quickly become known as one of the brightest and most promising legal minds in the West.

"We had talked about going to San Diego or San Francisco to live," Cassandra said. "Or maybe I should change that to I talked about it. You see, I've never liked this town."

"But you stayed because of your husband."

"Yes, he made all of this seem perfectly beautiful." Cassandra looked at Jessie as she knelt before the safe. "Why didn't he marry you?"

"Because he must have known someone wonderful like you would come into his life," Jessie told her.

Cassandra's eyes filled with tears, and she had to scrub them away with the back of her hand in order to spin the combination numbers on her husband's safe. When the door opened, she rummaged around for a moment and then she pulled out a file and stared at it. "This must be the one."

She handed the manilla file to Jessie, who opened it to find a single sheet with names written in Warren's neat handwriting. Jessie studied the names for a long moment; she did not recognize a single one of them.

"Here," she said, "do you know these people?"

Cassandra took the list, and for a brief moment she seemed unwilling to look down at the paper that shook ever so lightly in her hands. But she finally did force herself to look at the names, and Jessie could see by the way her eyes grew wide with shock and surprise that it was obvious she knew several of the suspects.

"This can't be," she said. "Some of these men are highly respected."

"And others?"

"A few are outlaws and killers, but they're still in the penitentiary where my husband sent them. And the rest . . . the rest I've never even heard of."

Jessie tried to hide her disappointment. "Every name on that list was added for a good reason," she said. "We both know that Warren would never have added a single name without having a strong suspicion that there was at least a possibility that one of them was the Arizona Strangler."

"I can't believe it," she said, pushing the list at Jessie. "Arnold Beard is a friend! And Jess Whitlow is the sheriff of Yuma!"

The poor woman looked so shaken and upset that Jessie did not want her to consider the names any more this day. She helped Cassandra up and led her back into the parlor.

"We can talk again tomorrow at greater length," Jessie said, folding the list up and placing it deep into her pocket. "I haven't had a bath or a clean dress on for over a week, so I think I'll go now."

"How inconsiderate of me!" Cassandra said, jumping up from her seat. "Let me offer the use of my—"

"No," Jessie objected mildly. "I'd really prefer a hotel room, and I'm sure that I can stop by and buy a few things very quickly. I'll be back tomorrow."

"For lunch," Cassandra said. "And I promise to be more helpful. I'll think more clearly about those names—every one of them."

"Good," Jessie said, "then we'll begin what has to be done tomorrow."

Lieutenant Jason Caldwell poured the last drop of wine in Jessie's glass. "Did you enjoy dinner? You sure did eat heartily."

Jessie brushed back her hair. She felt alive again, a new woman after a bath, a new dress, and what had turned out to be an excellent dinner with a superb California wine.

"Dinner was wonderful," she said. "I was famished, and I can't seem to get enough liquids inside of me to replace what I lost in the desert."

"Dehydration can be fatal in this heat," the doctor said. "I insist that every soldier drink at least a gallon of water a day in the summertime. But right now, I insist that you share a bottle of champagne with me."

"Isn't all this rather extravagant considering that U.S. Army lieutenants aren't paid a princely salary?"

"I couldn't survive for a week on my monthly army pay," the lieutenant confided. "You see, I am very fortunate to come from a rather well-to-do Boston family. They are generous enough to supplement my base army salary to the extent that I can enjoy the few luxuries available in Yuma."

Jessie smiled. "I see. Do you also come from a line of physicians? Or perhaps the Caldwell family has a rich military tradition."

"Both," Jason admitted. "My father served with distinction under General Ulysses Grant and his father was also a war hero. I'm not blessed by exceptional courage or even good fortune, and I think the times where battlefield greatness is required has passed. Out here in Arizona Territory, the war is fought in small, dirty skirmishes between the army and the last of the Apache. There's no glory in a thousand soldiers winning some pitiful victory over a few hundred starving Apache."

Jessie noticed a touch of bitterness in his voice. "If you really feel that way," she asked, "then why don't you simply resign your commission and take up private practice?"

"And break my father's and grandfather's hearts?"

71

He shook his head. "I'm not quite ready for that yet. They think that I'm fighting Indians on the frontier, little realizing that the commander of Fort Yuma believes that his only surgeon is too valuable to go out on campaign with the fighting men. So I stay here and patch up those that survive long enough to reach my little hospital. I also spend a good deal of time holding the hands of the officers' wives. I deliver babies, treat consumption, remove ingrown toenails, that sort of thing."

"You sound bitter," Jessie said as she watched a bottle of champagne arrive at their table.

The lieutenant uncorked the bottle and poured the bubbly liquid into their glasses. "To adventure, but not death, to mystery, but never betrayal," he said in toast.

Jessie drank and her eyes regarded him for a moment and she said, "You toast to mystery, and yet, you've not asked me why I came through the Sonoran Desert during the height of summer and while the Apache are threatening."

He chuckled. "That's the mystery I've been thinking about," he said. "You would not believe the wacky reasons I've imagined to account for your arrival at Fort Yuma. All of them wildly improbable."

Jessie leaned forward so that her face was near him. There were other diners in the room and she did not want her words to be overheard. "I'm here because of the death of Warren Hastings."

Jessie then proceeded to tell him about the letter, and finally she showed the young doctor the list of seven names. "Can you eliminate or elaborate on any of these men?"

Jason Caldwell's excitement was almost palatable. "You can eliminate Oscar Montoya and Art Logman."

"Why?"

"They're both in the Yuma prison serving life sentences for murder. They're cold-blooded killers, but even if they were out on parole, I'd rule them out because they are gunfighters, not stranglers."

Jessie scratched the two names out. "I understand that Jess Whitlow is your sheriff."

"That's right, so you can take him off the list."

"But why would his name be on it in the first place?"

"Beats me. Oh, he's got a reputation as being a 'shoot-first-ask-questions-later' kind of lawman, and I'm sure that's true. But he's not the kind of man who would strangle his enemies; instead, he'd ventilate them."

Jessie's eyebrows knitted. "I think I'll still pay the man a visit and see why Warren added his name to the list."

Caldwell shrugged his shoulders. "Suit yourself. I see you've got Arnold Beard down on the list. He's an attorney the same as Warren Hastings was. There's not a reason in the world why he'd have anyone killed."

"Maybe he was jealous of Warren and wanted his title and position."

"Maybe," Caldwell conceded. "I'm sure he'd like to possess Mrs. Hastings."

"What about the rest of these names on the list? Do you know them?"

"I've heard of them," the lieutenant said. "John Miller lives in Tucson and is a banker, and Hilton Turner is a fire-brand editor of the *Tucson Gazette*. He's always up to his neck in some kind of controversy. This last fella—Ike French—I've never heard of him."

Jessie studied the names. Except for Ike French, she at least knew who the names belonged to and where these men could be found. "You've been a lot of help."

The lieutenant sipped his champagne. "Do you really think that Cassandra Hastings is in danger?"

"Yes," Jessie said. "I think that Warren was a man who would not make that kind of a judgment unless there was something behind it. I also think that each of these men is somehow related to the Arizona Strangler. It's a puzzle and I wonder if I'll be able to find the solution before someone else is murdered."

"Why are you telling me all this?" the lieutenant asked.

"Because I might need your help if things get dicey."

"You've got it!" He reached across the table and took her hands in his own. "I think a little night air would clear our heads, don't you?"

"Sure," Jessie said. "After a wonderful dinner, wine, and this excellent champagne, I think a walk is exactly what I'd most enjoy."

"Good. It's still pretty warm outside, but we can stroll down by the river where the air cools off the river and you can see moonlight on the water."

Jessie was happy to get outside, and they walked arm in arm down to the Colorado River. The river was wide but, at this time of year, not very deep. In the spring it often flooded because of the tremendous thawing that took place high up in the Rocky Mountains, whose western slopes drained into this mighty river. By this time of year, it was almost low enough to walk across.

"It's still hot and kind of muggy," Jessie said, standing beside the gentle river. "I'll bet that water is cool and would feel wonderful to swim in."

"You can't imagine how good it feels," the lieutenant said. "Would you like to go for a swim?"

"You mean . . . now?"

"Sure! We could undress, swim, come back here and dry off in the sand, and then redress and be back to town without anyone even suspecting we finally managed to cool off."

74

Jessie giggled. The wine had relaxed her and the idea was definitely appealing.

"Come on," the doctor said, unbuttoning his tunic and then sitting down to pull off his boots. "I'll never tell anyone."

Jessie's resistance crumbled under the force of his boyish enthusiasm. "All right," she said, turning her back and unbuttoning her dress. A moment later she heard a splash as the lieutenant dived into the river.

"It feels wonderful!" he yelled the moment his head surfaced. "Come on!"

Jessie peeled out of her dress, underclothes, shoes and stockings. She felt ridiculous standing naked in the moonlight with a man she hardly knew, and when she turned and started toward the water, he whistled with admiration.

"Why, Jessie!" he exclaimed. "You're built like a Greek goddess!"

In answer, Jessie dived neatly into the river and swam underwater for almost a full minute, feeling the strong current pull her downriver and enjoying the chill of the snow-fed river water. When she surfaced, she swam to shallower water before wading back upriver to a bar of sand that was submerged by only a couple of inches of water. Jessie wiped her face dry and watched the army doctor come swimming over to her side.

"I told you that you wouldn't regret coming in here with me," he said, sliding in close so that their hips touched.

Jessie turned to him. "There were times this past week on that hot, dusty road from El Paso that I never dreamed I'd feel cool again, much less feel the caress of cold water on my skin."

He touched her shoulder and she shivered, and then they kissed. His mouth was hard and insistent, and Jessie found that she wanted him very much. He slid over her body, cool and easy in the water. His mouth left hers and found her nipples and teased them until they were hard and her breasts ached with the heat of her desire.

Jessie leaned back and spread her legs apart.

He lifted his head. "What's the matter, don't you even want to go back to shore?"

"No," she told him. "I want you right here in the river."

He chuckled and when his stiff root poked at her eager womanhood, Jessie grabbed his buttocks in both hands and pulled him deep inside of her. "Take me slow, Doctor," she ordered him. "We're in no hurry."

He pushed up on his arms and looked down at her while his narrow hips began to rotate and his manhood stirred her like a big spoon. "You are incredibly beautiful," he panted, watching the muscles of her stomach, hips, and thighs contract and relax as she milked him with her body. He kissed her again, and she felt his thrusts become a little more urgent.

Nearby, a big catfish splashed in the shallow water, and Jessie's fingernails bit deeper into his thrusting buttocks. She could feel the sand swirl around her as their exertions grew increasingly more frantic, and she thought that she could not get enough of his manhood, so she rolled him over and began to pump up and down on his stiff rod until suddenly he cried out with pleasure and she felt herself being lifted up in the water as he filled her with his seed.

Jessie lost control of her body, and a moan welled up from deep inside of her as his mouth again found her breasts and his hand slipped between her legs and joined his thrusting rod to bring her to a shuddering climax that seemed to go on and on until she groaned and rolled off of him, finally satisfied.

The lieutenant sat up and pulled her close to his side. "Yesterday," he said, gazing up at the moon and stars, "I thought my life was wasted in this hellish place. Today, you arrive and everything has changed. Your presence has changed hell into paradise, Jessie."

In reply, she kissed him hungrily. "I'm going to need your help as well as my samurai's if I'm to have any chance of uncovering a strangler before more people are garroted to death."

"You've got it," he said. "Because I'm the only doctor in Yuma, I pretty much do as I please. I've got a lot of freedom to come and go."

"Good," Jessie said, running her hands over his broad chest and strong legs. "Because I may need to keep you busy day and night."

He smiled, kissed her lovely breasts, and slid back between her legs. "I'm going to especially enjoy the night work," he said, rubbing his manhood between her legs and delighting her when it grew hard again so quickly. "I think that, for this poor army officer, it's just what the doctor would have ordered!"

★

Chapter 7

Ki studied Jessie's face with a half smile of amusement. "You look a little tired this morning," he said. "What's the matter, isn't the bed to your liking at the Horizon Hotel?"

Jessie knew that her samurai suspected she had spent the night with the handsome army doctor, but he would really have been amused to know that she had also spent a good deal of the night in the cool current of the Colorado River. "I had some trouble sleeping," she said, "but I'm sure I'll do better tonight."

Jessie and the samurai often teased each other about their romances. Both she and the samurai had a perfect understanding never to intrude into each other's love affairs.

Jessie and Ki were standing out on the boardwalk near her hotel. Already, the day was very warm and Jessie knew that it would get a lot hotter before the afternoon was done. "I want you to return to Tucson," she said. "After what we've been through in order to get here, I'm sorry I have to ask you to do this, but it's very important."

The smile of amusement slipped from his face. "You know that I do not like to leave you unprotected."

"Yes, I know that very well. However, I'm sure that I will be safe here. And if there was some threat on my life, Sergeant Wakefield and Lieutenant Caldwell are very close."

The samurai's concern was not diminished. No one could protect Jessie as well as himself, and both of the men she had mentioned were quartered at the fort, which was a good half mile from the Horizon Hotel. Much too far away to help Jessie in an emergency. Ki knew full well that, in his absence, Jessie would be working day and night to uncover evidence that would reveal the identity of the Arizona Strangler. It stood to reason that her efforts would be noted and her own life would soon be in jeopardy.

"What do you want me to do in Tucson?"

"There are two men that we found on Warren's list of suspects. Their names are John Miller, who is a successful banker, and a Mr. Hilton Turner, who is an editor."

"They don't sound like stranglers to me," Ki said.

"No," Jessie admitted, "they don't. And I'm very reluctant to send you off with almost nothing but their names and occupations. But if Warren placed them on his list of suspects, then there had to be some reason. As you remember, there have been a number of stranglings, and they have occurred throughout Arizona Territory. That tells me one of two things are taking place. Either the Arizona Strangler is a loner who travels around this territory on some kind of a vendetta, or there is some link between all the players on that list."

"What possible link could there be?"

"I have no idea." Jessie surveyed the distant prison walls. "I've heard about that place," she said. "It's supposed to be like a hell on earth at this time of year. This whole town seems somehow dangerous. Its citizens are worried about the Apache, and I'm sure that the prison is a constant and grim reminder of what might happen if there was ever a riot and the inmates staged a massive breakout."

"That probably has a lot to do with why the army post is here," Ki said. "But yes, I've been mixing with the people since we arrived, and there is a pessimism that goes beyond the threat of the Apache."

"The thing that impresses me," Jessie said, "is that Warren chose to settle in this town. I guess he probably felt that it needed him more than any other place he'd seen."

Ki turned and looked toward the east. He really did not want to return to Tucson, but understood that he must. "I'll leave on the next stage," he said. "And if they've stopped running, I'll buy a horse and leave tonight anyway."

Jessie reached into her pockets and handed the samurai a hundred dollars. "Whatever you do, be careful," she told him. "If John Miller and Hilton Turner really are involved in these stranglings, then they will be formidable opponents, one being a banker and the other an editor. I don't have to tell you that having control of the press and the money in town gives those two an enormous amount of power. Also, I spoke with the sheriff when we passed through last week, and he did not impress me as the kind of man who would be very helpful if things go against you."

"Yes, I recall that was your impression. But when we went to visit Mrs. Hale, whose late husband was a judge who'd been murdered by strangulation, I felt that she was a woman that would be very useful."

"That's true," Jessie said, recalling the sixty-year-old widow who had served them a delicious drink of papaya and orange juice. "What was the name of the ex-convict that she thought might have been the real killer of her husband?"

"Joe Hagan," Ki said.

"Yes! Talk to Mrs. Hale again. Seek her cooperation. Ask her about the banker and the editor and dig up whatever you can find."

"I will. And what should I do if I discover who the Arizona Strangler really is?"

"Don't do a thing until I can contact someone that I know is incorruptible and then make sure that the strangler is going to pay in full for his heinous crimes."

"It's hard to know who to trust in this business, isn't it?"

"Yes," Jessie said. "The sheriff of Tucson did not seem helpful, but neither did I get the impression that he was nervous or hostile, as a man would be if he had something to hide. I think you'll find the sheriff honest, but ineffective."

"Is there anything else I can do in Tucson?"

"No," Jessie said. "But I think you ought to wait a few days to recover from what we just went through."

"With your permission, I'd like to leave at once. The sooner I reach Tucson and complete my investigation, the sooner I'll be able to return and protect you."

"All right. Just be careful!"

"A samurai does not need to be worried about," he said. "It is you that concerns me most. Are there any suspects you found on Warren Hastings's list that live here?"

"Yes. But two are in prison and the other is the sheriff, a Mr. Jess Whitlow."

"If anything happens to you before I return," the samurai said as he turned to leave, "those men are going to have more grief than they ever believed was possible.''

"Nothing will happen to me," Jessie called as the samurai headed for the stage office to see if there were any more runs to Tucson.

Jessie waited until the samurai emerged from the stage office and shook his head at her to indicate that all scheduled stagecoach runs between Tucson and Yuma had been suspended. She bit her lip with worry and watched the samurai head off toward the stable to buy a good horse. Then, knowing that she had her own work cut out for her, Jessie turned and walked down to the sheriff's office and entered.

"Howdy!" the sheriff said, jumping out of his swivel chair and smiling when Jessie came through his door.

Jessie appraised the man swiftly. Sheriff Jess Whitlow was in his late twenties, tall, broad-shouldered, and prematurely balding. It was already hot in his office, and his face was slightly flushed but his smile was disarming. He sure didn't look like the kind of man that should have been included on Warren's list of suspects, but then, looks were darn near always deceiving.

"Have a seat, Miss . . ."

"Starbuck," she said. "I'm a friend of Mr. and Mrs. Warren Hastings. I've come for a visit."

"Well, you sure couldn't have picked a worse time to come to Yuma," the sheriff said. "I'm sure you know all about the Apache trouble in these parts."

"I came to be with Mrs. Hastings in this time of her mourning," Jessie told him.

"Of course you did!" the sheriff said, realizing his observation had been rather thoughtless. "Say, can I get you a cup of coffee? Just made a new pot yesterday."

"No, thank you."

"Okay, so what brings you to my office?"

Jessie studied the man a moment and decided not to be evasive. She'd shock this grinning lawman so badly that it would be nearly impossible for him not to show his true feelings.

"As you know, Warren Hastings was brutally strangled to death. What I want to know is, what have you done—if anything—to apprehend the murderer?"

Sheriff Whitlow's eyelids shuttered and his smile turned brittle. "I guess you have a right to ask that question," he said after a long beat. "But I don't much care for the way you asked it."

"I'm not here on a social call," Jessie said. "I want the murderer caught and tried for the strangulation of Warren Hastings."

"Then you might have a damn long visit because I haven't a clue as to who strangled Warren," the sheriff said. "The county prosecutor was a good man, but in the courtroom he was responsible for a lot of men being sent to Yuma Prison. Now, as far as I can see, any one of them that was sentenced and has been paroled just might be the one who strangled Hastings."

"And how many would that be?"

"Beats the hell out of me." The sheriff poured himself a cup of coffee. "Miss Starbuck, I'd say there were at least thirty men that were prosecuted by Hastings for crimes ranging from murder to horse thievin'. Most of them are still in that territorial prison yonder, but some are out on parole."

"You should have tracked those that were released down and questioned them," Jessie said.

"And *you*," Sheriff Whitlow said, his anger getting the better of him, "should stick to whatever the hell it is you do besides meddle into matters that are not your business."

Jessie was glad the sheriff was losing his temper.

Maybe, if she got him angry enough, he might also say something that would be helpful. "Sheriff, did you know that Warren Hastings left a list behind of the men that he suspected were candidates for the suspect he called the Arizona Strangler?"

The sheriff's jaw dropped. He snapped it shut and then stormed, "Hell no, I didn't!! If he left behind a list, why wasn't I told about it by Mrs. Hastings?"

"Because she was not aware that such a list existed until I arrived yesterday. And we then opened Warren's safe and found it."

The sheriff started to say something, then seemed to think better of it and clenched his teeth so that his jaw muscles stood out in relief.

"What's wrong?" Jessie asked. "Aren't you even curious as to whose names were on the list?"

"Sure I am! In fact, I demand that you hand the damned list over to me right now."

Jessie shook her head. "I don't think that would be very wise at all. But I'll tell you something you'll find highly interesting."

Jessie paused a moment and then hit him right between the eyes. "Sheriff, your own name was on that list."

"What!" He staggered.

"You heard me," she said. "Your name was on the list!"

"Sonofabitch! Hastings and I never did get along, but I never thought the man was so lowdown he'd stoop to the level of calling me a strangler. Me! The sheriff of Yuma!"

Jessie studied the man closely. Was his anger and outrage real, or just a very good acting job? She could not be sure, but it seemed to her that Sheriff Whitlow's anger was more bluff and bluster than genuine outrage. She decided that this man was definitely a candidate, and she was very glad that she had not given him Warren's list.

"I need to know the other names!"

"Find them out for yourself."

"If I can't get them from you, then I'll damn sure get them from Mrs. Hastings! I'm the law in Yuma. You can't hold back evidence!"

"It's not 'evidence' at all," Jessie said. "It's just a list of names."

Sheriff Jess Whitlow was livid, and Jessie figured that she had said enough to prod the man into some kind of rash action. If he was a part of some sinister plot to assassinate important men in the Arizona Territory, then perhaps his rage would make him reckless. If he was not guilty in any way, then he would eventually settle down and start thinking clearly enough to realize that he needed to do far more in order to apprehend Warren's murderer.

Either way, Jessie thought, I've put things in motion here. And now, it's just a matter of seeing which direction the hot Sonoran winds will blow.

After leaving the sheriff's office, Jessie went straight back to visit Cassandra Hastings and explain what she had done and why. Cassandra listened carefully, then said, "You've sort of placed your neck in the noose, don't you think?"

"I don't know what to think," Jessie admitted. "What are your impressions of Sheriff Whitlow?"

"My husband didn't have much liking or respect for him, I know that much. He said that there was something strange about Jess. Something that just did not ring true."

"But he never gave you any specifics?"

"No," she said. "He did not. As best I can recollect, Warren had several run-ins with Jess over how evidence and testimony were to be used during the prosecution of criminals. But he never said anything more than that. You see, Warren thought that I'd worry about him too much if I knew what he was doing. I worried anyway. It does not take a woman of great imagination or intellect to understand that a prosecuting attorney, in these days and times, can make a lot of deadly enemies who may later seek revenge."

"I see." Jessie shook her head. "It would be exactly like Warren to try and shield you from worry. And quite frankly, I'm also worried for your safety, just as your husband was."

"But why should I be in any danger?" Cassandra asked. "I played no role in the prosecution of criminals."

"Yes, but what if someone thought that your husband might have confided in you about his investigations? If they did, then it is reasonable to suppose someone whose guilt has not yet been revealed would be very nervous about you."

Jessie bit her lip. "And with my arrival, I'm afraid that their anxiety and determination to insure that you cannot possibly incriminate them will increase."

Cassandra stood up and began to pace up and down her parlor floor. Her brow was knitted, her hands were clasped behind her back, and Jessie thought it best to simply allow the woman to think in silence.

Cassandra finally seemed to reach a decision. She halted before the window and gazed out at the Colorado River. "If what you are suggesting is, in fact, a reality, then my life certainly is in danger. However, if I run as I think you are suggesting, then I do nothing to draw out the man or men who murdered Warren. But if I stay, I might just be able to force their hand."

"It's a very dangerous game you are suggesting."

"Life itself is dangerous. I've heard what happened to you and Ki trying to reach Yuma. I had no idea what a sacrifice I was asking you to make when I wrote you at your Texas ranch. Because of my blind selfishness, a passenger, a guard, and the driver of your stagecoach were killed by the Apache. I feel completely responsible."

Jessie stood up from the chair she had been using and walked over to Cassandra Hastings. "You aren't a bit responsible. The drummer would have taken that stagecoach whether or not we were going. He was obsessed with the idea of winning back his wife's heart which had been stolen by some California alfalfa farmer."

"Poor, poor man," Cassandra said.

"And the others were free to make their own choice, though I suppose Ki had something to do with making the guards decide to continue west from Tucson."

"Do you think Ki will be all right going back there?"

"I haven't a doubt in the world," Jessie said. "Ki is vulnerable only when he is worried and trying to protect me. When he is responsible only for his own safety, he is at little risk. If the Apache make the mistake of attacking Ki on the road back to Tucson, they will pay for it with even more lives."

"He is *that* deadly?"

"Yes," Jessie said. "He will teach the Apache a few more tricks if they meet. And when he reaches Tucson, he'll waste precious little time investigating those two men whose names we found on your late husband's list of suspects."

Cassandra nodded. "If I am in danger, then so are you. Jessie, will you move out of the Horizon Hotel and stay with me until all this is finished and the Arizona Strangler is caught and either hanged or imprisoned?"

"If it would make you feel safer, then yes," Jessie told her. "I daresay that anyone who came looking for trouble would have more trouble than he bargained for in this house between the two of us."

Cassandra brightened. "I know how to handle a gun," she said. "Warren insisted that I learn, so we would drive to the outskirts of town just up the river and practice shooting at floating sticks and cans that we'd throw into the current. I daresay I am a pretty fair shot."

Jessie smiled to encourage the woman even though she was not greatly impressed. Shooting sticks and cans floating down the river was one thing—shooting a man who came in the night to strangle you to death was quite another.

Lieutenant Jason Caldwell was going to be very unhappy indeed when he discovered that she had moved in with Cassandra. It meant they would not be able to continue their late-night rendezvous on the Colorado River. At least, not nearly as often.

"I'm so happy you're moving in with me!" Cassandra said. "I can't tell you how lonely and afraid I've been since Warren died."

Jessie put her arm around the lovely young widow. "We're going to spend more time practicing our shooting," she vowed. "And we're going to make sure that this house is sealed up tighter than a corset on a fat lady."

Cassandra giggled happily. But Jessie, thinking of how she would not be able to enjoy the pleasures of midnight skinny-dipping and lovemaking with much regularity, simply smiled. There was much to do, and if Sheriff Jess Whitlow really had played a part in Warren's tragic death, then it would take all her cunning and skill to gather proof against him and to keep both herself and Cassandra alive.

Jessie thought of the samurai who would be leaving Yuma within a few hours on the way back to Tucson. She was going to miss him very much, and even though she had given the impression

88

that Ki was invincible, that was not entirely true. In hand-to-hand fighting, he was invincible. But against either an assassin's or an Apache's bullet, even a samurai could be slain.

★

Chapter 8

Ki had bought the best horse that could be found in Tucson along with a saddle, bridle, horseblanket, and hobbles. The saddle was old and had only cost him ten dollars, but the horse was young, a five-year-old strawberry roan that had long legs and a deep chest that promised it could run far and long without becoming winded. Ki had gladly paid fifty dollars for the gelding, and after he'd bought a few supplies, he still had money left in his pockets.

The samurai brought his weapons, too. The bow and his quiver of arrows, his *shuriken* blades, and the wooden nunchaku which could be very valuable in close fighting. The nunchaku consisted of two heavy sticks about a foot long that were attached together at one end by a few inches of braided horsehair. The one that Ki preferred and usually carried was called *han-kei,* which was simply a half-sized version only about seven inches long and flat on one side so that the sides fit perfectly together.

The *han-kei* was easy to carry and easy to conceal. Ki kept it hidden in his jeans and could whip it out in an instant. Holding one of the sticks, a trained samurai could whirl the other stick with enough force to stun a bull. He could also perform virtually every *te* block and strike, and the *han-kei* gave each blow a tremendous force. As the *han-kei* whirled it actually made a low whirring sound and when the hard wood struck an opponent, it cracked bones. Ki could also use this weapon to crack an opponent's joints much like a nut in a vise.

The only weapon in Ki's arsenal that he did not bring on this dangerous journey back across the Sonoran Desert was his *bō* or staff. Being five feet long, the *bō* was simply too cumbersome to use with great effect from horseback.

"You're a damn fool to head back to Tucson with the Apache on the warpath," the liveryman who'd sold Ki his horse and saddle commented. "Now mind you, what a man does is his own business, but I sure hate to think what would happen to that pretty roan horse if he falls into Apache hands. They use them down to skin and bone and then they roast them, you know."

"I know," the samurai said as he mounted. "But if this animal is as fast and strong as you promised, the Apache will never catch me."

"Oh, they'll find a way if they see you," the man drawled. "They send smoke signals to their friends up ahead and they'll cut your escape off. And just remember, they know all the water spots in that desert and you don't."

"I appreciate your concern for the horse," Ki said. "I'll try to see that he doesn't get roasted."

"I'd appreciate that. I raised him from a colt, and if you'd told me that you were riding him to Tuc-

91

son, I'd have refused to sell the animal. Fifty dollars is top price, but I got a soft spot for that gelding.''

''When I return, I'll give you the first chance to buy him back,'' the samurai promised. ''And I'll even let you make a little profit on the deal.''

''Hell, he won't be worth much after runnin' to Tucson and back.'' The liveryman walked over to a tack box and pulled out a big skin water bag. He filled it in his watering trough, and it must have held ten gallons of water because he could barely lift it up to sling it over Ki's saddlehorn. Next, he brought a gunnysack half full of grain and tied it to the other side of the saddle.

Ignoring the water that was leaking down the samurai's pants, the man said, ''Sure, there's a lot of weight there, but it could save the gelding's life.''

Ki was amused. ''Not to mention my own.''

''Like I said, you're the fool in this game and you'll probably get scalped about like you deserve. It's the—''

''I know, I know,'' Ki said. ''It's the horse that you're worried about. Well, I'll tell you what. I'll bet you double or nothing that I bring him back in good condition. If I do, he costs you one hundred dollars. If I don't . . .''

The feisty liverman didn't let him finish. ''. . . then you'll be scalped buzzard bait out on the desert somewheres and I'll never see you or the roan again. No deal.''

''Suit yourself,'' the samurai said. ''But don't say I didn't give you a chance.''

Ki rode out of Yuma with the sun going down. He purposefully rode past Mrs. Hastings's house, and both Jessie and Cassandra were out on the porch to say good-bye.

''Nice horse,'' Jessie said with admiration. ''I'll bet you had to pay a great deal for him.''

''Fifty dollars.''

"He's worth a thousand times that much if he keeps you ahead of the Apache," Jessie said, giving the samurai a large roll of bills.

"I don't need all this money," Ki complained. "Why, there must be four or five hundred dollars here."

"You didn't look very close," Jessie said. "There is better than five thousand dollars."

The samurai was stunned. "But why?"

"When you reach Tucson, I want you to buy a western suit of clothes and some expensive shirts, ties, and boots."

The samurai's eyes widened with disbelief. "You know I hate western clothes!"

Jessie was firm. "Ki, listen. I want you to present yourself as being exactly what you are—my agent. I want you to go to see that banker, Mr. John Miller, and tell him you represent me and I'm interested in buying property around Tucson. A lot of property."

"But it's all cactus and sage!"

"Never mind that," Jessie said. "Tell him that you've come to look over real estate, and then you spread this money around as if there was plenty more to come. Also, make sure that Tucson's editor, Mr. Hilton Turner, hears about the story. He'll want to interview you."

"What am I supposed to tell him?" the samurai asked. "That you've decided to go into the jackrabbit-raising business?"

"Don't be ridiculous. Tell him a little about Starbuck Enterprises. If he's like most small-town editors, he'll have visions of new wealth, new opportunity, and new subscribers buying his paper. He and the banker will probably fall all over themselves to please you."

Ki sighed. "I see what you're saying and I guess I would have a lot better chance of investigating them if I seem to have money and power behind me."

"Of course you will. If you ride into town looking poor, you won't get the time of day from either man. Feed their natural greed."

Ki was not too excited about the plan, but he knew that it made good sense. "I'll wear a suit, but I'd be useless wearing those pointy-toed boots and a necktie. I wouldn't be able to breathe or run at all."

"What about your long hair?" Jessie asked. "I don't suppose you'd consent to a regular haircut?"

Ki shook his head adamantly. "Jessie, you know I'll gladly give my life to save yours. But what you're asking is worse than death. If my hair is still intact by the time I reach Tucson, then I want to keep it. The banker and the editor will just have to deal with me in a western suit and we'll leave it at that. I think all this money will carry the day."

Jessie reached up on her tiptoes and grabbed the samurai around the neck and kissed him on the cheek. "You take good care of yourself. I don't know what I'd do without you."

"I'll be back," he promised. "But until I do, I'll worry about you every waking minute. Be careful—both of you ladies."

Cassandra nodded; she looked a little teary-eyed at the prospect of the samurai riding off to what she considered would be less than even odds to survive.

Ki touched his heels to the roan and galloped away with the huge, sloshing water bag almost throwing the gelding off stride with its great weight.

He'd make it all right. He'd wear the damned suit, and if the banker and the editor were somehow tied up in this strangler thing, then he'd put them permanently out of commission, one way or another.

Ki expected a run-in with the Apache, and yet he was determined to avoid one if at all possible. So he traveled by night and by noon the next day, he and the roan were hiding in the shade of boulders. Ki fed the gelding a generous bait of oats and poured a gallon of water into a basin of rock. The gelding drank greedily while Ki hobbled the animal and climbed the rocks to study the country up ahead.

It pretty much looked all the same to him. Just more cactus, brush, and rocks. He had decided not to follow the stagecoach road back to Tucson, knowing full well that the Apache would be watching it very closely. But when a man decided to strike out across this rough country and forge his own trail, he was also taking a sizable risk that his horse would clip a cholla cactus and go lame, or throw a shoe, or even get bitten by a rattlesnake.

The air was very still and heat waves undulated off the hills. Ki surveyed every inch of his panorama but saw nothing that indicated the Apache were somewhere up ahead.

He was tempted to push on, but he resisted the idea knowing that he had to pace the roan and save it just in case its speed was called into play. So the samurai went back down under the rocks, and after kicking a tarantula out of the way, he lay down and closed his eyes. Sleep came easily to him in the smothering heat, and when he awoke, the sun was just sinking into the western horizon.

Ki poured more water into the rock basin, fed the horse a second helping of oats, and resaddled the animal. He mounted and reined the fine gelding eastward, knowing that he would ride all night in comparative safety.

But at about five o'clock in the morning, he saw what he was sure was an Apache campfire burning about a mile ahead of him on the desert, and he knew that there was going to be too little time to skirt the camp before full daylight. Ki had no choice but to seek a hiding place before the camp up ahead came alive. This was sure as hell no kind of country to be caught flat-footed in.

There were no big rocks that Ki could see, so he

pushed the willing roan closer until he reached a deep arroyo which he rode down into and dismounted. Hobbling the animal, he crawled up the side of the arroyo and watched the campfire until he saw Apache beginning to move about. The samurai counted five Indians. In a few minutes he heard a shot and then watched an Indian pony fall and quiver in death. It was quickly butchered, and very soon Ki could smell the strong stench of scorched horsemeat.

The roan smelled it, too, and tossed his head nervously. Ki went back down into the arroyo and calmed the frightened animal, and when he was sure the roan would not try and run, he crawled back up to see the Apache all seated around their morning campfire eating. The samurai was just about to glance back down at his horse when he noticed the white woman. She had blond hair and was sitting off by herself on a rock. When a barrel-chested Apache approached and offered her a piece of horsemeat, she shook her head and turned her face away.

This seemed to infuriate the Apache, who grabbed her face in his hands and twisted her head around. He forced the meat into her mouth and she spat it out. The Apache was furious. He drew his hand back and hit the girl so hard she flew over backward off the rock she'd been sitting on. Then the Apache grabbed her by the hair, took the dirty meat the woman had spat out and shoved it into her mouth.

Ki watched as the woman was forced to choke the dirty meat down while the powerful warrior held her head back and placed a knife to her throat as the other Apache watched.

The woman nearly choked to death trying to swallow the lump of half-cooked horsemeat. Even from a half mile away, Ki could hear her wretching and choking. But finally the woman managed to swallow the meat and then she spat in the Apache's face.

Ki almost cringed because he knew that the girl

was begging to be shot or tortured. Instead, the Apache, who seemed to have a claim on her, lashed out with the flat of his hand and knocked her flying. This time the girl did not get up and the Apache turned and proudly walked back to the campfire, where he speared another piece of meat and ate it with obvious relish.

Ki slid back down the arroyo a few feet and considered what he should do next. His allegiance was to Jessica Starbuck alone and yet . . . yet he knew that she would not want or even expect him to do nothing for the captive white woman. A young woman who had probably been kidnapped from some ranch after her husband had been filled with Apache lead or arrows. A young, very brave and very foolish woman willing to starve to death rather than live as an Apache slave.

Ki frowned. He would have to rescue the woman, and that meant he would shadow the Apache until nightfall and then try to reach her sometime in the night.

Ki edged back up to the lip of the arroyo and waited until the Apache finished eating and then broke camp. They saddled their thin ponies and rode away, the white woman astride a pinto with a rope connecting her slender neck to the hands of her owner.

Ki watched the Indians for almost an hour. They were moving south toward Mexico, and Ki wondered if the Apache were going to sell or barter the white women for money, liquor, or guns.

The samurai slept for three hours in the arroyo until the sun became unbearable. He then arose to water the roan and grain it heavily before he rode it out of the arroyo. The roan moved at a steady trot for the next two hours. It was soon covered with lather, but as far as the samurai could tell, it wasn't breathing a bit heavily.

At midday Ki found more rocks and sought the relief of shade until early evening, when he again took up the trail of the Apache. The Indians made no attempt to hide their trail because, despite being constantly hunted by the United States and Mexican armies, they were the lords of this desert kingdom.

It was almost midnight when the samurai finally dismounted less than a quarter of a mile from the Apache camp. Their fire had burned low and Ki stayed even lower as he crept forward with his *tantō* blade in his right hand and his *han-kei* in his left.

Ki stopped at the edge of the campfire and studied the sleeping figures. When he saw the woman's yellow hair, he slipped soundlessly forward. It was his intention to take the woman and steal the Apache ponies. The woman and the barrel-chested Apache were lying close together and Ki knelt by her side before he clamped his hand down hard over her mouth.

The woman awoke with a scream building in her throat. She looked up at the samurai and saw only his long hair, dark skin and the braided leather headband. No doubt thinking that she was about to be assaulted by one of the Apache, she bit Ki's hand and her scream filled the air.

Ki spun on his heel and his thin *tantō* blade flashed once, burying itself into the chest of the man who had claimed this woman. The other Apache seemed to spring off the ground and attack with bloodcurdling screams.

The *han-kei* whirred in a deadly circle and as the warriors threw themselves at Ki, the heavy wooden sticks smashed heads, arms, and faces. Apache warriors reeled in pain as the samurai took the fight directly to them and the *han-kei* did exactly what it had been designed centuries ago in Japan to do— knock men senseless. One Apache, smarter than his peers, grabbed a rifle and brought it up to fire, but a foot-strike to his midsection sent the warrior reeling and the whirring *han-kei* soon found and broke his skull like a thin eggshell.

The fight lasted but seconds. Two of the Apache, severely disabled, crawled off into the brush and Ki let them go.

"Who are you!" the woman cried.

"Never mind that. Let's get their horses and get out of here!"

The woman did not have to be told twice. She found rope halters, and they sprung on to the narrow backs of two ponies. Ki led the way, driving the other ponies on ahead until they came to the place where he'd hobbled the roan.

The samurai dismounted the thin pony he'd stolen and remounted his gelding. "Follow me!"

"Who are you?! Where are we going?!" she cried.

Ki stampeded the ponies eastward. "Tucson! And right now, all I want to do is put some distance between us and those Indians before they regroup and decide to come after us."

"But you killed three of them! And the two that lived were running for their lives when they lit out into the brush."

The samurai slowed the horses. "All right," he said. "Maybe we don't need to hurry. But it is entirely possible that the pair that survived might send smoke signals and tell their friends to prepare a surprise party for us."

The woman was silent for almost a full minute before she said, "Whoever you are, you're dead right. But who the hell are you?"

"I'm a samurai," Ki said.

"A what?"

Ki explained as best he could, though his mind was very much of the fight he'd just won and the possibility that they might have to battle their way

99

through more Apache before they arrived safely in Tucson.

"My name is Rose Hagan," she said. "I was prospecting in the mountains south of Tucson when the Apache showed up."

"Prospecting? All alone out there by yourself?"

"Sure. I had my burro with me, but they ate the poor little devil."

Ki clucked his tongue with sympathy. The young woman was filthy and her face was banged up pretty good. She smelled rank, and if there had been water in this country, she would have been a prime candidate for a bath.

"Isn't it a little risky for a woman to be out prospecting all by herself?"

"Not anymore than for a man to be riding across country and then figure he can sneak up on an Apache camp and live to tell about it. I'm sure grateful that you were so foolhardy, though."

"Thanks," Ki said, unsure whether or not he'd been insulted or complimented.

"What's your name?"

"Ki."

She frowned and wrinkled up her nose. "Ki? Hell, that's no kind of a name. I'm gonna call you Hero. You mind that?"

"Yes."

"All right then, Ki it is. But when we reach Tucson—if we get across this damn country and reach it alive—then I'm going to buy you some American clothes and Stetson hat and a—"

"Hold on now!" Ki had just remembered that he was supposed to change his image. "As a matter of fact, I'm going to buy a western suit and all the trimmings."

"Good. I'll help you pick out something just right. I could use a dress and a few doodads myself."

100

Ki didn't say anything, but he sure wished that he wasn't riding downwind of her just now. Her name might be Rose, but despite her courage and her obviously cheerful nature, she smelled pretty much like a skunk.

★

Chapter 9

The stiff-necked tailor cleared his throat and said,
"You call yourself Mr. Ki?"

The samurai nodded. This man irritated him, but
he was supposed to be the best tailor in Tucson.
"That's right. And I'd like to buy a suit of clothes."

The tailor frowned and studied the unusual man
who stood before him. He noted Ki's loose black
tunic and pants, his long hair and sandals. "I think
you might be in the wrong establishment. Don't you
think you would be more . . . more comfortable in
something . . . uh, like you're wearing?"

"Of course I would," Ki said, pretending indig-
nation. "But as I explained, I was robbed and some
heathen took my suit, tie, new shoes—everything—
and left me with these clothes."

"How terribly unfortunate," the tailor said. "And
you say that you are a representative of whom?"

"Miss Jessica Starbuck of the great Circle Star

Ranch and Starbuck Enterprises.'' Ki scowled at the man. "Can we dispense with the questions and get on with the fitting?"

"Of course, of course! First, I need to take measurements."

Ki frowned but said, "All right. Go ahead."

The tailor, whose name was Mr. Teagarden, pulled a tape measure out of his own perfectly tailored coat. Teagarden was a dandy and looked as if he'd stepped off the pages of a mail-order catalog from New York. His black suit was accentuated by a white shirt, black silk vest and a black tie.

"Now," Teagarden said, "if you'll lift your arms up, please."

Ki did as he was requested, but the moment the tailor reached around his chest, the man jumped backward. "My God!" he whispered. "What on earth are you carrying under your clothes!"

Ki lowered his arms, remembering he was still carrying his *shuriken* star blades. "Listen," he said, fully out of patience now. "When I entered your store, I noticed that you did have some suits already made. And since I am in somewhat of a hurry, I'd like to buy one if I can find a reasonable fit."

"But Mr. Ki! Those suits are really not the finest, and a man representing someone like Miss Starbuck—a name that is respected even in Arizona—should not compromise his tastes."

"Well," Ki said, moving over to the rack of suits. "There are times when we all have to compromise a little in life. And this is one of them."

The samurai picked out a suit that appeared to be about his size, and he took the coat off the hanger and tried it on. It did fit though the arms were a little too long. A few minutes later he tried on the pants and they were a little long also. But the shoulders and the waist measurements were correct, and the

103

samurai had been around Jessie and her wealthy associates long enough to recognize quality.

"Can you make the alterations and have this brought to my hotel room at once?"

"But of course! The Baron House?"

"Of course," Ki said. "Room two fourteen."

The tailor smiled. "And what about the haberdashery?"

"The what?"

"Your accoutrements. You know, shoes, stockings, belt, tie, shirt, cuff links and so on and so forth."

Ki bumped his forehead with the palm of his hand. "Of course! Listen, pick out two of everything and send them along with the bill."

The tailor beamed. "Very good, sir! You may rely on my excellent taste and discretion."

"I'm sure that I can."

"And," the tailor said in the same breath, "if you will forgive me for asking for a small deposit right now."

Ki pulled out the roll of bills and peeled off two hundred dollars. "This ought to do it."

Teagarden's eyes grew round with joy, as well they should have considering that the average working man would never pay more than twenty dollars for a suit and five dollars for a pair of shoes. "Oh, yes, Mr. Ki! And I think that the bill will not exceed this even by one penny."

Before Ki could warn him that the bill had better not exceed two hundred, Teagarden dropped to his knees and, holding his breath, measured Ki's dirty feet. A second later, he popped up and wrapped his little tape around the samurai's neck.

"Just making sure," Teagarden said with an ingratiating smile.

Ki turned his back on the man and walked out the door. He spied a barber shop and hesitated. He ran his hands through his dirty, shoulder-length hair and across the prickly whiskers of his jaw. Ki wore a thin mustache and it was getting downright bushy. "What the heck," he said. "It'll be harder to impress a banker and the editor than it was that tailor."

With a great deal of reluctance, Ki crossed the street and entered the barber shop. It was empty except for the barber who looked at Ki and said, "I don't serve Chinamen."

"I'm not a Chinaman, you idiot!"

The man blinked because no Celestial ever spoke to a white man in that manner.

Before the barber could recover enough to work up a rage, Ki said, "My name is Mr. Ki. I have already suffered a narrow escape from the Apache, and I will not tolerate insolence. I want a trim, a shave and I want it quick. Here!"

Ki shoved ten dollars at the barber, and the money washed away the last glimmer of an already dying protest.

"Yes, sir, Mr. Ki! A trim and a shave, coming right up!"

Ki walked out an hour later with a lot less hair than he had expected, and he was very displeased. His hair no longer touched his shoulders, and in fact, did little more than cover his ears. When he had seen himself in the mirror, he'd been aghast at his shorn appearance. Why, Rose would hardly recognize him when he took her to dinner.

But the hair was gone and Ki knew that there was nothing that could be salvaged by throwing a fit, so he left in a silent rage. At the Baron House he was greeted by the same hotel desk clerk he'd tipped twenty dollars.

"Good day, sir!"

"Good day," Ki said abruptly.

"I gave your wife an extra key," the clerk said cheerfully. "She's taking a bath upstairs. Poor woman must also have suffered terribly along with you during the Apache attack.''

Ki stopped in mid-stride. "My wife?''

"Yes, Mrs. Rose Ki. Is . . . is there something wrong?''

"No,'' Ki said quickly. "Thank you. I'll have more bath water brought up, please.''

"Yes, sir, Mr. Ki.''

The samurai hurried past and then took the stairs two at a time. Damn that Rose anyway! She'd told him she was going to be staying at a boarding house. And now . . . now she'd brazenly moved in with him as his wife! The trouble with that was that someone in Tucson was bound to see and recognize her. That would completely blow his credibility. Well, she'd made her bed, now she'd just have to stay hidden in the hotel until this whole charade was finished.

Ki was furious when he opened the door, then slammed it behind him. Their spacious room was the best the hotel had to offer. Red velvet curtains. A huge, four-poster bed. Original oil paintings depicting mission life in the Southwest, even a few potted cactus plants on a small balcony overlooking the main street of Tucson.

"Rose!'' he shouted, moving through the room into the bathroom. "Rose, I thought . . .''

Whatever he had thought was forgotten when he saw her standing in front of the mirror, her long blond hair clean and smelling like shampoo, the dirt scrubbed off her face, ankles, and arms. She turned wearing only a smile. "Hell, Mr. Ki! Welcome to marriage and the good life!''

"But I hadn't intended to pretend I was married!''

Rose shrugged, and despite his anger Ki could not help but noticing she was a very well endowed and shapely young woman. She came tiptoeing wetly across the Spanish tile floor and smiled as she kissed his freshly shaved jowels. "Ummm, nice. Why don't you take a bath and then we can discuss this entire matter over the bottle of champagne I've ordered from the bellman."

Ki shook his head and grinned. "You really know how to take advantage of an opportunity, don't you, Rose?"

"One like this does not often come along in a poor girl's lifetime."

"Poor girl? I was under the impression you had a little pile of gold hidden away somewhere out in the desert."

"Well, I do," she said quickly. "More than a little, actually. But I will have to buy another burro and a prospector's outfit when all this charade is over. And besides, you understand that it's ever so much more fun spending someone else's money. I hope Miss Starbuck does not object."

"She can live with it," Ki said. "But . . ."

A knock on the door interrupted his flow of thought, and when he answered it, four grunting bellmen came in with another huge tin tub of hot water. "In there," Ki said, then quickly added, "No, wait!"

Ki hurried into the bathroom. "Cover up," he ordered. "If you're going to be my wife, you've got to at least pretend some modesty."

Rose giggled, found a bathtowel, and waited while Ki ushered the four sweating bellmen inside. Her dirty bathwater was taken out and his was left in its place.

Ki glanced at Rose, shrugged, and undressed.

"Oh, my!" Rose said, clapping her hands with delight. "You are nice!"

He blushed, climbed into the tub, and sank in the hot water up to his chin. A samurai was not supposed to ever completely give himself in to worldly pleasures, but Ki decided that, for the next few hours, he was going to do just that.

"May I scrub your back?" Rose asked.

"Sure."

Rose found a body brush and knelt by his side. Ki tried to close his eyes again, but the vision of her lush, exposed breasts only a few inches from his mouth would not go away. So he took the brush away from her and said, "Why don't you join me?"

"It is big enough for two," she said, "but I just dried off and . . . aw, the bellman can bring us up all the damned towels we're going to need, can't he?"

Ki pulled Rose in with him. The tub overflowed across the Spanish tile, but he did not care, especially when Rose parted her legs and knelt over him. Her right hand found his rod and her left hand found a bar of scented soap which, with a pixieish smile, she used to work him up to a stiff lather.

"So big, erect, and clean," she said, tossing the soap aside and positioning herself so that he could penetrate her whenever he wanted.

Ki held his hips motionless as his lips found her breasts, which tasted a little soapy still but he was not about to complain. She arched her back and her head rolled to one side, and she sighed with pleasure as his tongue teased her hard nipples.

"Ummm," she whispered.

Ki felt her hands slide under his hips and then she rocked her own hips down hard on his. He growled and his fingers bit into her soft buttocks as he clamped her down hard on his throbbing root.

Rose moaned, squealed, and hugged his neck.

"Take it easy," he said, "I'm slipping underwater!"

But Rose was already lost in pleasure. "That damned Apache that took me was like a rabbit," she panted. "He was so rough and fast. But you, oh, Mr. Ki, I'm going to suck you up like a licorice stick!"

Ki pushed his feet against the tub to keep his head

above water. He'd hated to leave Jessie in Yuma, but until he finished his own investigation, this was going to be all right!

Rose began to pump so hard that bath water was sloshing all over the tile and to keep her from emptying out all his hot, clean water, Ki rolled her over and pinned her to the tub, then pleasured her until she roared with delight and her legs drummed the walls of the tin tub.

Only when her body spasmed and then went limp did the samurai allow himself release and he took her with his own great urgency.

It took Rose several minutes to catch her breath. "Good heavens!" she breathed. "I think you might have to order some more bath water!"

Ki stood up, then pulled Rose to her feet, where she swayed weakly against his chest. "If you get out, I'll wash and meet you on the bed and we'll take it a little slower."

She got out. "Oh, boy," she whispered, "are we going to have a good time as long as this party lasts!"

For some reason, Ki just laughed. And then he sat down and washed himself from his shorn locks right down to his toes while Rose combed her long, blond hair.

"Rose," Ki said when he stepped out of the tub, "you're going to have to stay in this room or my story about being here to represent the Starbuck empire just isn't going to fly."

"I know that," she said. "These people in the hotel are of no concern because they never saw me before." Rose shrugged her pretty bare shoulders. "I never stayed in a place like this until now."

"Do you know the late Judge Hale's widow?"

"Nope." Rose frowned. "Why should I?"

Ki toweled off and then walked into the bedroom, stretched out on the bed, and sank his head into

109

the feather pillow. Without going into great detail, he told her about the Arizona Strangler, why he and Jessie had risked their lives to reach Yuma, and why Jessie had asked him to hurry back to Tucson.

"Judge Hale was also strangled just like Warren Hastings. We think there is some connection. Mrs. Hastings and Jessie found a list of two suspects that live in this town. They are none other than Tucson's editor, Mr. Hilton Turner, and one of its most powerful bankers, Mr. John Miller."

"I know them well enough," Rose said. "They'd smile with their faces covered with cowshit. I never liked either one, but they don't seem to be the kind of men who'd be in on some plot to strangle judges and prosecuting attorneys."

"Well," Ki said. "They are on the list and that's why I'm here and forced to pose as an investor for Starbuck Enterprises. There's another name that comes into this."

Ki had to rack his brain a minute. "Oh yes, the widow Hale mentioned that her late husband's ring was stolen by his murderer. It has five diamonds."

Ki went to his clothes and rummaged around inside a pocket until he dug out a piece of paper. "Mrs. Hale drew a sketch of the ring and the man she believes is the one that really strangled her husband."

"Let me see," Rose said, coming over to stand beside the samurai as he unfolded the sketch and smoothed it out over the bedspread.

"Uhhhh!"

Ki glanced up to see that Rose's face had drained of color. "What's wrong?"

"That's my husband!" Rose whispered. "He disappeared years ago and I thought he was dead."

Ki studied the girl's face. "What is his last name?"

"Hagan, same as mine."

110

Ki took her arm and set her down beside him. "Maybe you had better tell me all about Joe Hagan."

"He was wild," Rose said, her eyes distant and her voice so low that the samurai had to lean close to hear her. "The first time I saw him was out in the desert. I was in trouble with the Indians again. Three of them had me pinned down in the rocks and Joe came by and killed them all. He was my hero—like you, Ki!"

The samurai said nothing and waited for her to continue.

"But unlike you, Joe was bad inside. I fell in love with him before I realized that, and I married him three days after he saved me from the Apache. Of course, like a love-struck fool, I told him where my gold was hidden. He stayed with me about a month, then left me broke and alone. He took my gold and lit out for New Mexico Territory, and I understand he started robbing banks. He came back to Arizona and shot a marshall, and finally he was caught and sent to prison."

"And was he sentenced by Judge Hale?"

"Yes. And Mrs. Hale was telling the truth when she said he threatened to kill her husband. I was in the courtroom when he said it only one of dozens of times. Anyway, he was sent to prison for life. He killed a guard there and escaped. I heard he died in a gunbattle several years ago over in Tombstone."

Ki stared at the sketch. Joe Hagan would have been a handsome man except that there was an unmistakably cruel expression on his thin lips, and Mrs. Hale had given him a nasty scar over one eye.

"Is this the way he looked the last time you saw him?"

"Yeah. He was a handsome devil, wasn't he?"

Ki studied the sketch for another moment and then he folded it up and put it away. "What will Joe Hagan do if he runs into you?"

"After he rapes me . . . or before?"

"After."

Rose sighed. "He'll probably have some cock-and-bull story all made up as to why he never tried to find me. And when I take a swing at him for stealing my cache of gold, he'll have an excuse for that, too."

"And then what?"

"He'll want me back for a while. But I'd rather die first than trust that snake again."

"It sounds like your husband is the kind of man who'd not hesitate to kill you if you refused his wishes."

"That's probably true."

Ki stood up and paced back and forth. "As far as you know, did your husband have anything to do with either the editor or the banker whose name I mentioned?"

"He went through school with both of them. They were childhood friends," Rose said. "Joe used to always laugh about how the three of them were always getting into mischief."

Ki stopped his pacing. At least now he had established that all three men were friends. "Do you have any idea why the names of the banker and the editor would be on Warren Hastings's list of suspects?"

"No," Rose said. "Joe has killed plenty of men, and though I'd never have figured he'd strangle someone, it's possible. But Mr. Miller and Mr. Turner, well, it just doesn't fit."

Ki lay back down on the bed. Rose was correct . . . but only up to a point. What seemed more and more apparent to the samurai was that the Arizona Strangler was probably not operating on his own. If Joe Hagan was the strangler, then it was entirely possible that he was working for men of power and influence—people like bankers and editors who stood to gain a lot by manipulating politicians, judges, and

112

lawmen. And if those kind of people refused to be manipulated, it stood to reason that they would be eliminated.

"Eliminated," Ki said, thinking aloud, "in a way so heinous that the act would be thought to have been committed by a man insane . . . or crazed with hatred."

"What?"

Ki snapped back to the present. "I said that the reason people have been strangled is simply to give a false lead. Nothing more."

"Oh."

Rose folded up against the samurai. "What happens if my husband finds out that I'm up in this room?"

"I don't know," Ki said. "According to what you told me a few minutes ago, he'd come up to rape you, then take you away."

Rose sat up fast. "And I said I'd rather be dead first."

"It won't come to that," the samurai said. "I won't let that happen. But if you should ever run into him, I want you to find out what he and his two playmates are up to."

Rose was silent for a long time and then she said, "I guess if I could do that, then the mystery would be solved."

"That's right," Ki said. "But even if you never see Joe again, I'm going to pay a visit to the banker and the editor, and I'll get to the bottom of this mystery, and I'll do it before a week has passed."

Rose nodded. Her color was coming back, and now she moved up close to the samurai and pushed him back on the bed. "I don't even want to think for the next few hours. I just want to feel. Can you help me?"

Ki cupped her large breasts in his hands and nodded. "I think I know exactly what you need to distract your mind from the shock it's just received."

His tongue found her nipples and she moaned and wiggled all over like a stroked puppy. Ki pushed her down on the bed and mounted her swiftly, but then he began to take her very, very slowly.

★

Chapter 10

The next morning Ki stood before the full-length bathroom mirror and scowled at his reflection. "I hate these western-style suits," he growled. "Where am I supposed to hide my *shuriken* blades or my *tanto* knife? Or the *han-kei*?"

"If the *han-kei* is that pair of nutcracker sticks, then I'm afraid you're out of luck. But maybe you can slip those cute little star blades into your inside coat pocket."

Ki reluctantly tossed the *han-kei* aside and slipped the blades into the coat pocket. The necktie and starched white shirt were killing him, as were the shiny new shoes that pinched his toes.

"Quit grimacing so!" Rose said with a laugh. "You look wonderful."

"I feel like I'm wearing a straight-jacket," Ki complained. He stepped back and attempted a few hand strikes and then a foot strike, which damned near tore out the seam of his new trousers.

"If an enemy jumps me, then I'm going to be in serious trouble," he said with a sad shake of his head.

Rose moved to his side. She straightened his tie and handed him a new leather attaché case. "If it makes you feel any better, put your big nutcracker in here."

Ki did that and then he kissed Rose and headed for the door.

"Who are you going to see first?"

"The banker," Ki said. "I'm supposed to be an investment representative."

"Think you can pull it off?"

"Of course I can," Ki said as he opened the hall door. "I've sat through a hundred or more financial meetings with Jessie. I know the terms and the protocol. I can talk investments and high finance, though neither subject is of the slightest interest to me."

"Pretend interest," Rose said, blowing him a kiss. "And when you come back, bring food, champagne . . . and lust."

Ki had to laugh. "Lock the door and don't try and seduce all the bellmen before I return," he said.

Ki walked down the hall, descended the stairs, and moved through the lobby, feeling the eyes of several other businessmen appraising him with interest. When he reached the hotel's ornately carved front door with it's beveled glass, he caught an image of himself in the glass, and it reinforced the impression he had that he looked very rich and successful.

And why shouldn't he, dressed in such an expensive suit and shoes and with his hair cut neatly and his mustache trimmed to a pencil line?

Outside, he took a deep breath and headed for the

bank that was managed and partly owned by a Mr. John Miller. Ki had earlier rehearsed his introductory explanation, and he figured that he was ready.

Inside the bank he did not waste time by going to the rear of a line of people waiting for some clerk to handle their transactions, but instead he marched right up to a closed teller's window and rapped sharply on the glass.

A young banking clerk snapped to attention. He saw the Oriental-looking Ki and his brows knitted with annoyance. "You will have to take your place at the end of the line," he said. "Just like everyone else."

"What is your name!" Ki demanded imperiously.

The clerk blinked. "Why . . . what . . ."

Ki had the young man slightly off-balance, and he had no intention of allowing him to recover. "I said, what is your name!"

"It's Winfred P. Scott," the young man stammered, "and just who—"

"I will have to speak to Mr. Miller about your rude behavior. I demand to see him at once."

Ki certainly had the young man's full attention now. "And who are you, sir?"

"My name is Mr. Ki and I represent the Starbuck Enterprises. I don't expect that to mean anything to a lowly bank clerk like yourself, but I do expect it to mean a great deal to Mr. Miller. Now, will you bring the man to me, or shall I take my investment money elsewhere?"

"Uh . . . no, no. I'll get Mr. Miller. Please hang on just a moment."

"Thank you!"

Ki watched the clerk, who could not have been twenty, dash into a spacious office upon whose glass door was Mr. Miller's name followed by the word *President*. The samurai had disliked having to be so abrupt with young Scott, but there were certain occupations that seemed to respect arrogance and bad manners and to consider politeness a lack of self-confidence. In Ki's estimation, bankers and their underlings fit into that classification.

The samurai could see Scott gesticulating and then John Miller appeared in the doorway. He studied Ki for an instant, then smiled, and that was the instant that Ki knew he had passed the first great hurdle. Bankers were not only arrogant, they were naturally suspicious.

Scott rushed out of the bank president's office and said, "Mr. Ki, Mr. Miller will see you, but he has an appointment at eleven o'clock."

Ki glanced at the big clock near the front door. It was ten-thirty. If he did not have John Miller completely hooked in thirty minutes, he had lost the game anyway. "I understand perfectly. Without an appointment, I probably cannot expect his full morning's attention."

Scott flashed a nervous smile, lowered his voice, and said, "I never heard of that Starbuck Enterprises, but Mr. Miller definitely has. I'd appreciate it if you'd not say anything about my initial rudeness. I really—"

"Let's just forget about it," Ki said in a confidential manner.

Scott visibly sagged with relief as he opened a little swinging door to allow Ki to pass out of the lobby into the offices of the bank. "Thank you very much!"

Ki walked past him without another word. When he came to Miller, he hesitated until it was Miller who extended his hand first and then Ki took it and said, "I apologize for the intrusion, but I've been told on excellent authority that you are Tucson's most prominent banker, and so I determined to start here."

John Miller was a very tidy-looking man dressed

118

in a dark suit. He wore gold, wire-rimmed glasses and a heavy gold watch and chain. His jowls were so closely shaven they were shiny, his hair was parted down the middle and oiled. The banker's shoes sparkled and his fingernails were manicured. He looked like a man better suited to the high society circles of Boston rather than to being engaged as a frontier banker.

"Well, thank you," he said, his lips just managing a smile. "Mr. Scott said you represented the Starbuck Enterprises. Is that so?"

"Yes, Miss Jessica Starbuck is the reason I am here now," Ki said. "She is interested in real estate."

"In Tucson?"

"That is correct."

"Come into my office, Mr. . . . . Ki, was it?"

"Exactly." Ki took a chair across from the bank president's huge desk. The office was plush but much too ostentatious for a man of real wealth and good taste.

"Now," Miller said, "what kind of real estate are we talking about? I know a little about the Starbuck saga, about Miss Jessica's father and everything. And I know she has an enormous cattle ranch in central Texas. This is not good cattle country, as I am sure you can see."

"Miss Starbuck is not interested in buying cattle," Ki said. "She is more interested in commercial property."

The banker frowned. "Whatever for?"

"For investment purposes. What else?" Ki asked, relaxing.

Mr. Miller frowned, then leaned forward. He selected one of three freshly sharpened pencils laid out for him and he began to doodle on a pad of paper as he spoke. "This is my home," he began, "but frankly, were I an international power in the world of trade and finance—as I understand your employer

119

to be—then I should certainly not be thinking of investing money in Tucson.''

''Why should you, of all people, say that?''

The banker smiled with self-deprecation. ''I'm just being frank with you, Mr. Ki. And I find it very difficult to imagine that the great Starbuck Enterprises cannot find better investment channels and opportunities than here in Tucson. As you know, we are not even able to quell a vicious Apache uprising.''

Ki shook his head tolerantly as if he had just heard the objections of a child. ''Miss Starbuck is a world investor and a force to be reckoned with in every major financial market. And it's true we have vast holdings on every continent. However, it is often true that the opportunity we sometimes overlook is the one right under our own noses. In this case, Miss Starbuck believes Tucson offers a remarkable opportunity.''

''Why?'' the banker asked very bluntly. ''I live here, and while I certainly don't believe this town is going to wither up and blow away or be overrun by the Apache, I also don't see that much opportunity. If anything, we've lost population these past few months. Trade and commerce are both practically at a standstill because of the Apache and—''

Ki interrupted by saying, ''All that you say is true, but very temporary and minor aberrations that are taking place before a major boom in this town. Why do we say this?''

Ki paused a moment, watching the banker's intentness. He had spoke to Jessie before coming here, and she had given him a few inside facts which he was about to use in order to spring a trap on the banker.

''Mr. Miller, I'm sure you are aware that the new and exciting Tombstone and Bisbee mineral discoveries will very soon exert a decidedly beneficial effect on Tucson's stagnant economy. An impact

120

that will bring new wealth to this community. We also believe that the Southern Pacific Railroad could be induced to begin construction into this town much sooner than originally planned."

"Who has told you that?" The banker had stopped doodling and was leaning forward. He was suddenly very attentive.

Ki paused as if he were carefully considering whether or not to divulge some magnificent secret. "Miss Starbuck, as you know, has worldwide connections, some of which actually are of national importance. Because of that and her very influential friends in Washington, sometimes she is privy to things that others might not be privy to."

Ki flashed the banker a smile. "Are you understanding me, Mr. Miller?"

The man's chin dipped up and down. "Oh, yes! At least, I think so. But I was told by the Southern Pacific management as recently as last year that they would definitely not reach Tucson until 1880."

Ki chuckled. "I think that those plans might be a little too conservative. In fact, I believe, if the right . . ." Ki winked conspiratorially. ". . . if the right connections are made, that the railroad might come several years earlier. And if that happens—as Miss Starbuck is sure that it might—then there would certainly be a land boom. The Southern Pacific people have also intimated that they would be very interested in building a great railroad yard and extensive railroad shops in Tucson. The railroad's arrival, coupled with the ore discoveries I've already mentioned, would cause real estate values to soar, wouldn't you agree?"

"My God, yes!" Miller whispered. "Land would quadruple overnight. And right now, with this Apache trouble, land owners are willing to practically give their commercial and residential properties away."

"Of course they are," Ki said with a patient

121

smile. "And we both know that this little Apache problem is only fleeting. The day of the free-roaming Indian is already over everywhere but in the Southwest. The Eastern seaboard tribes have been either annihilated or subjugated, the Plains Indians are now conquered, and in my country, the Comanche and the Kiowa are no longer a threat. Believe me, the Apache are already beaten and simply do not realize it yet."

John Miller rocked back in his big office chair and steepled his slim, immaculate little fingers. "If what you say will happen, then this information you are giving me is worth . . . millions."

"Of course it is," Ki said happily. "And the Starbuck Enterprises has a history of being generous with those who are its friends. And I'm sure that you want to be our friend, don't you."

It was not a question, for Ki had no doubt that his trap had caught this banker mouse.

"Damn right, I do!" Miller exclaimed. "If you can get the Southern Pacific to come in here in a few years, it will put Tucson on the map and change the status of Arizona from a territory to a state!"

Miller cleared his throat and attempted to curb his boyish exuberance. "But you must understand that I alone cannot help you to the extent that you need to be helped. "How *do* you need to be helped?"

Ki shrugged. "Oh, I think you must know the people who have properties which represent—shall we say—real opportunities for investment."

"Oh, yes!"

"Good. Of course, you might want to bring in a wealthy friend or two to share in the good fortune. We are not greedy, Mr. Miller."

"Well, no," the banker said. "I can tell that already. And as a matter of fact, I do have an associate or two. Men who are silent partners in this

122

bank and who would be very grateful for your generosity.''

"Of course," Ki said. "And their names?"

John Miller hesitated for a minute, but under Ki's steady gaze, his hesitation wilted and he said, "Our editor, Mr. Hilton Turner, is one."

"Excellent!" Ki said. "The press can be very useful. Who else?"

"Actually, there is only one individual, and he lives in Yuma."

"I need to know his name so that we can coordinate our moves."

Miller nodded. "His name is Arnold Beard."

Ki did not betray his glee. Arnold Beard was the successful attorney that had been on Warren Hastings's list of suspects. "Very good," the samurai said. "Two associates. Is that all?"

Miller hesitated, then said, "Yes, I think so."

Ki smiled. "Mr. Scott said that you have an eleven o'clock appointment. I don't expect you to break it for me so I'll excuse myself and we can pursue this further at your convenience."

Miller popped out of his chair. "Well, listen, I can break that appointment. It's nothing that important. And—"

"I wouldn't dream of inconveniencing you," Ki said, coming to his feet. "Why don't we meet tomorrow and discuss this in greater detail? In the meantime, you can be thinking of getting us a city map with the names and legal descriptions of their owners. Tomorrow, we can study the map and plan our strategy. And if you would like to invite your editor and associate, Mr. Turner, then by all means, please do so."

The banker did not want to end the meeting, and there were dollar signs in his eyes. But Ki had seen Jessie handle this kind of greed often enough to know that you always left the player across the table from you wanting more.

Ki extended his hand. His tie was killing him, and the shoes were starting to make his feet ache. He could hardly wait to get back to the hotel and undress and then relax with Rose until tomorrow.

He bowed slightly and then said, "Good day!"

"Good day to you, Mr. Ki! And thank you for stopping by. I'm sure that we are going to have a very, very beneficial relationship."

"I never doubted it," Ki said, leaving the office and allowing Scott to open the door and let him out of the bank offices.

The samurai never looked back as he left, and it was well that he did not for he was grinning hugely. His only regret was that Jessie could not have seen him play this game which her father had perfected and had taught his lovely daughter.

Well, Ki thought, I believe some of the Starbuck business wizardry must have rubbed off on me, too.

★

Chapter 11

Ki watched Rose standing beside the window. She had not moved in almost fifteen minutes and Ki sensed her longing to go outdoors. He stood up from the bed and went to her side. "You're going stir crazy in this room, aren't you?"

Rose turned and laid her head against his chest. "I am," she admitted. "We've been here . . . what, a week? And while this suite is beautiful and the room service has spoiled me for work, I feel like a caged animal. I have to get out and stretch my legs. I need to smell the sagebrush and talk to people and live like a human being."

"But not just yet," Ki said. "There are bound to be plenty of people here in Tucson who recognize you. Someone is going to start asking questions, and when they discover you are pretending to be my wife, well, the game is up."

Rose sighed. "How much longer will it take?"

"Not long," Ki promised. "I've gotten to know both the banker and the editor, and they've started to borrow heavily in order to buy up commercial property all around town. They're both greedy and up to their necks in this thing."

"What about the Arizona Strangler? Are they behind the murders?"

"They're definitely a part of something. They and that Yuma attorney, Arnold Beard. It isn't yet clear why they had Jessie's old friend along with several others killed."

"And my husband, Joe Hagan?"

"I don't know what to think about him," Ki confessed. "Every time I've mentioned his name to someone in this town, they sort of clam up and walk away. Or else they look at me like I'm some kind of crazy even to want to know anything about him."

"Joe has that effect on people," Rose said.

"Well, from what I gather, he's alive and may even be somewhere in this town. But what he does or where he can be found, that's the question. One thing is sure, Miller and that editor must be keeping him under wraps."

Rose had another theory. "Joe might be out on a job," she said.

Ki had thought of that, too. "I've got to find him. He's the key. I can financially ruin John Miller and Hilton Turner, but that won't make them confess to what's behind their role in this strangling business."

"I think it's a plot to make Tucson the state capital when Arizona gets statehood. And I'll bet that it has something to do with who are to be the first powerbrokers in office."

"I think you might have something," Ki said. "Politics is the one common denominator between the stranglings in different parts of the territory. I've been asking around and even the sheriff who was

126

killed was about to run for mayor. But until I find your Joe Hagan . . ."

"Or he finds me," Rose said quietly. "There's not much that gets by Joe when he's in this town. People either love him or hate him."

"If he isn't here now, he soon will be," Ki said.

Rose looked funny. "What makes you so sure?"

"Because, I'm going to rain on our banker and editor's parade this afternoon. And I think that they will decide that I might just need to be eliminated— permanently."

Rose wrapped her arms around Ki's neck. "Isn't there some other way?"

"I can't think of any. We both agree that Hagan is probably the strangler. And if I can't find him, then he's going to have to find me."

Ki felt the young woman tremble. "He's only a man," Ki whispered. "Just a man."

"He's a devil," she told him. "He's big and strong—much bigger and stronger than you are. And he's expert with a gun or a knife."

"He's a knife fighter?"

"Yes. He has killed many Mexicans in knife fighting and done it for sport. Down in Mexico, he is known as *El Cuchillo Grande,* which means 'the big knife.' "

"And on this side of the border, he is probably the man known as the Arizona Strangler." Ki took a deep breath and expelled it slowly. "Rose, when you pick a husband, you really pick a doozy."

Ki went to the bank. When he entered, everyone smiled and bowed to him and the young clerk named Scott practically dived for the gate to escort him back to the bank president's office.

"Ah, Mr. Ki!" the two men said in unison.

Ki nodded and shook their hands. In contrast to the banker, Mr. Hilton Turner, the editor, was tall and rumpled, and his hands were always smudged with printer's ink. He was an intellectual sort, but very cynical and inclined to write sarcastic editorials in his newspaper. Ki had learned that Hilton Turner was the black-sheep son of a wealthy Baltimore industrialist. He'd been run out of Maryland by his family and, for some unknown reason, had chosen to make his mark in Tucson. Ki had the impression that Turner was bitter and determined to make a quick fortune so that he could show his father how wrong he'd been to judge Hilton unworthy.

The banker had good news. "We've managed to buy that big parcel of sagebrush on the south end of town," he said with great excitement. "But we had to pay a ridiculous amount. It seems that our little . . . acquisitions are finally starting to create a lot of speculation. People are saying that we are about to make a killing."

Ki had been the one to leak this rumor and drive the prices of land purchased by this pair ever higher. "What did you have to pay?" he asked.

"A thousand dollars an acre," the editor interrupted, his voice filled with disgust. "Hell, a month ago it could have been had for a hundred dollars an acre."

"Never mind that," the banker said. "As Mr. Ki has said, when the Southern Pacific decides to build its new train yards there, we'll be worth a fortune."

Ki frowned. "I'm afraid . . ."

The banker wasn't listening and he was eager to tell all of his exciting news. "And we also borrowed enough funds to sign the deal on that real estate you suggested. It cost us nearly twenty thousand, but now we own all the water rights and we've got the Southern Pacific over a barrel. They'll have to deal with us at our terms and . . ."

Ki's face darkened as he feigned great concern. "Gentlemen," he said. "We had an understanding

128

that you seem to have forgotten in your rush to make a killing on real estate. Remember, I warned you to leave Starbuck Enterprises enough land so that we could also profit. Now, you seem to be telling me that you've gobbled up everything!''

"Now, wait a damn minute!" the editor said. "This is *our* town, not yours. We are the ones that have been here during the bad times, not Jessie Starbuck. And so we feel that local money and local investors should profit first and foremost. I'm sure that the Starbuck Enterprises will find a way to make their profits somehow. I don't worry about that at all. Hell, what's another few hundred thousand to a woman like Jessica Starbuck?''

Ki stood up from his chair. "That is obviously the way you see it," he said, injecting anger into his voice. "But I see it differently. I see two men . . . men I trusted to assist me and the Starbuck Enterprises to make a reasonable profit . . . who have allowed their own greed to interfere with their good sense.''

John Miller flushed with outrage. He was not accustomed to anyone telling him he was greedy. He made sure that his door was firmly closed before he said, "Now see here, Mr. Ki. I don't think that hurling accusations at each other will accomplish any useful purpose. And as for our buying up what you consider to be the most lucrative investment properties, well, you should have acted sooner. Business is business, man!''

"That's right," the editor snapped.

Ki smiled. "I think I am going to take the next stage back to the Circle Star Ranch, where I will advise Miss Starbuck not to invest in Tucson real estate because there is little profit left to be gained here. Furthermore, she will withdraw her influence upon the Southern Pacific and that will have the immediate effect of canceling their construction plans.''

Both the banker and the editor paled slightly, and Ki pushed the dagger deeper into their greedy, shrunken little hearts. ''Gentlemen, I am sorry to say that you have succeeded in ruining not only our joint venture, but also yourselves. Good luck with your new investment properties; you will need all the luck you can get.''

The editor jumped forward and grabbed the samurai's arm. ''Now, wait a minute!'' he cried. ''Are you saying that, without Miss Starbuck's influence, the Southern Pacific will abandon its plans to push a line into Tucson?''

''Of course not,'' Ki said, pulling his arm away. ''I am saying that they will simply delay those plans another five or ten years.''

The banker staggered. ''But that will be disastrous for us! We used every dime we had of our own funds, plus we borrowed to the limit. Not only that, but we paid inflated prices. If you do this to us, we'll both be ruined.''

''Yes,'' Ki said. ''You will be. Good day.''

The editor hurled himself at Ki, but the samurai easily ducked his fist and drove his hand into Hilton Turner's soft, bloated underbelly. The editor gasped like a beached fish and doubled up as the samurai straightened his tie and walked out the door.

''Mr. Ki,'' Scott said. ''What happened in there!''

Every person in the bank had seen the editor's outrage and attack and then the samurai's almost casual-appearing blow that had rendered the tall, rumpled man helpless. ''I'm afraid the Southern Pacific is not coming to Tucson quite as soon as those men thought it might,'' he said loud enough for everyone to hear. ''Too bad that they borrowed all your depositors' funds to make a quick profit that has now evaporated into thin air.''

Ki walked out the door knowing that his words would soon be repeated all over Tucson and that rumors would fly. Everyone would now realize exactly why their banker and their editor had been buying land, and they would be furious. Even worse, the value of land would fall drastically.

Mr. Miller and Mr. Turner would have only one recourse to take, and that would be to kill him before he could reach Texas. To do anything less would be to allow themselves to be driven out of Tucson in bankruptcy and disgrace, if they were not lynched by the angry townspeople whose money they had borrowed to finance their own greed.

As Ki walked toward the stage depot to inquire about the next eastbound stage, he could only imagine the consternation that must be taking place inside the bank he'd just left. There would be sheer panic in the hearts of both the editor and the bank president. It would probably take them a few minutes to recover from their shock, and then they'd rush to see Ki enter the stage depot. They would know when the next stage would leave, and Ki would bet anything in this world that they would send for the mysterious and deadly Joe Hagan, the one and only Arizona Strangler.

When Ki stepped into the stage depot, the only man in the room was a tired-looking old man who was working on some papers.

"Excuse me," Ki said. "But when is the next stage leaving for El Paso?"

"Not until the damn Apache will let it," the man snapped.

"I have to reach El Paso," Ki said.

The old man thumbed his green eyeshade up on his bald pate and stared at the samurai with unconcealed irritation. "All right, I've orders to dispatch an eastbound stage out on Friday," he said, "three days from now. But I don't guarantee that it will get

131

done. Not many men willing to drive a stage with the Apache raisin' hell. But if it goes, a ticket will cost you a hundred and thirty-five dollars one way.''

Ki pretended outrage. "But it was only thirty-five dollars to come here from El Paso!''

"That's right," the clerk said. "The extra one hundred goes for extra guards and extra hazardous pay. Take it . . . or leave it, mister.''

"I'll take it," Ki said, extracting the money from his wallet.

The clerk took the bills, counted them twice, and then gave Ki a ticket. "If the coach doesn't leave, you can get this money back on Friday. If it does run, then it'll depart at ten o'clock in the morning. If you're late, you lose your money.''

"Thanks," Ki said, pretending to be annoyed. "I'll be here.''

The samurai walked out outside, glanced surreptitiously at the bank to see Miller and Turner watching him, then strolled off toward his hotel knowing that, by Friday, he would either have killed Joe Hagan or been himself killed.

At least, he thought, by Friday Rose will be free to move about Tucson to her heart's content.

Later that very same afternoon a man rode out of town on a fast horse. Within an hour, he came to an abandoned gold mine. The very same one that had once belonged to Rose.

"Hello in there!" he called, his eyes panning back and forth across the desert country, always on the lookout for Apache. "Mr. Hagan, you in there?''

Joe Hagan stepped out into the bright sunshine. He was tall, well over six feet, and powerfully built. He was shirtless and his torso rippled with muscle. It was also laced with knife scars. The scar up on his brow was angry looking, and he was covered with rock dust. Behind him, a very young Apache girl

132

peeked fearfully out of the cave. She was bare-breasted and pretty but looked thin and exhausted.

"What the hell you want?" Hagan growled.

"They got another job for you."

"It'll have to wait."

"Can't wait until past Friday," the rider said, not wanting to argue with Joe Hagan but not seeing how he could ride back with any answer but that this man was going to kill Mr. Ki.

"How much this time?"

"Three hundred."

"That ain't as much as last damn time!"

The horseman forced an apologetic grin. "The bosses are damn near broke. They're in some trouble so it'll be a little harder for them to come up with the money. But it'll be half in advance, half when the job is done. Same as usual."

"Who?"

"Nobody you know. He's a funny-looking guy. About six foot, but slender, and he has yellow skin and slanted eyes."

"A chink!"

"Yeah, I think so. Only he's bigger and kind of different than most Chinamen I seen."

"The hell with it," Hagan snarled, starting to go back into the tunnel. "I ain't stooping so low as to kill chinks."

"You might when I tell you who he's living with at the Baron Hotel." The rider paused, then added, "He's livin' with your wife."

Hagan blinked. "With Rose?"

"That's right. How's it feel to have your own wife being screwed by a Chinaman?"

In answer Hagan jumped forward, and before the horseman could use his spurs, Hagan had him by the shirtfront and was dragging him out of his saddle. The horseman landed hard, and Joe Hagan landed on his chest with drawn knees, squashing the breath and the fight out of him.

Hagan drew a knife from his belt and placed it at the rider's throat. As the man's eyes bugged with fear, Hagan drew the knife across his throat until a thick line of blood appeared. The rider began to scream and beg.

Hagan shoved his blade into the man's mouth and hissed, "Scream once more and I'll cut out your tongue and let you strangle on your own blood."

The horseman, almost wild with terror, found a shred of reason and managed to shudder into silence.

"Now, you say Rose is sleeping with this chink?"

The horseman nodded, but in doing so, he cut his tongue on the blade. Sweat poured into his eyes and he could feel his heart banging in his ears. Joe Hagan had always brought fear to him, and now he knew that fear had been justifiable.

Hagan withdrew his knife. "What room are they in?"

"Two-fourteen. He's leavin' for El Paso on the stage come Friday. Mr. Miller and Mr. Turner want him dead first."

"Strangled?"

"I . . . I guess so. They didn't say. They figured you'd know."

Hagan climbed off the man. "You tell them to leave the money same place they did the last time. I'm gonna cut off the chink's balls, and then I'm gonna cut Rose so she ain't so pretty anymore. Now get out of here!"

The horseman scrambled to his feet and ran for his horse. The horse panicked and wheeled to gallop back toward Tucson. The horseman spun around. "Mr. Hagan, will you help me? If I get caught on foot out here . . ."

"Then kiss your dumb ass good-bye," Hagan

said, a wide grin splitting his dirty face as he guffawed loudly.

The horseman turned and went stumbling off in the direction of Tucson.

Hagan pivoted around on his heels and entered the mine shaft, his arm encircling the slender waist of the Apache girl. "I thought my wife had more damn good taste than to ever stoop so low as to screw a chink," he growled to the girl who giggled nervously because she did not understand English but did understand that she had better laugh at everything he said and service him however and whenever he wanted.

"A chink, for God's sake!" Hagan roared in anger as he dragged the girl deeper into the cave. "She's insulted me is what she's done. And nobody insults Joe Hagan and lives!"

The Apache girl's voice had a note of hysteria, and her forced giggling followed them back into the mountain.

Chapter 12

Joe Hagan watched Ki exit the Baron Hotel carrying a large paper sack. He measured the samurai with a contemptuous grin on his face, and then he angled for the back alley that would bring him up behind the hotel.

A few minutes later he was standing under the fire escape, and being tall and powerful, he had no trouble leaping up to grab the iron grate and haul himself upward. The fire escape was old and it squeeked with protest under his heavy weight as Hagan hurried up to the second floor. The door was locked against intruders but Joe had expected that because the Baron Hotel was a pretty fancy place. Standing on the fire escape, Hagan forced the big blade of his Bowie knife in between the door and the jam and gave the knife a series of powerful wrenches. The bolt pulled loose as he knew it would, and he entered the upstairs hallway and stood perfectly still until his eyes became accustomed to the poor light.

A few minutes later he moved down the hallway until he came to room 214. He pressed his ear to the door and listened. He heard Rose humming and his smile widened. She'd always liked to hum some damned tune, and it was kind of pleasant for the first few hours, but then it became damned grating on a man who enjoyed his peace and quiet.

Joe debated whether or not to knock on the door and attempt to trick Rose, or simply to bash the door down. He decided to trick Rose because she had always been a trusting woman.

Rapping lightly on the door, he called in a cheerful voice, "Room service."

He heard the humming stop and then the soft padding of Rose as she came to the door. The bolt turned and the door opened just as he had expected it to. Rose had a smile on her face that died like a shot animal when she saw Hagan. She opened her mouth to scream, and Hagan doubled up his fist and busted her flush on the jaw. She went down hard, and he stepped inside and closed the door behind him, then locked it.

Rose was stunned and he picked her up and dragged her to the bed. He tossed her on it and then he ripped her dress off and unbuttoned his pants. He was spreading her legs apart when she roused enough to realize what was happening and cried, "No!"

Hagan doubled up his fist but instead of submitting as he'd expected, she drove her fingers into both of his eyes, and he shouted with pain and smashed blindly downward with his fist. He felt his knuckles connect with her face and he hit her again, his own vision blinded.

"Damn you!" he roared, staggering back and crashing into a table, then almost falling.

He covered his wounded eyes with the palms of

137

his hands. The pain was unbearable, and he thought for sure that Rose had torn his eyes out. But after several minutes, the pain subsided a little, and he gingerly touched his fingertips to his eyelids. Satisfied that his eyes were still intact, Hagan opened them and saw the room as if through a waterfall. He swore again, staggered into the bathroom, and found a pitcher and basin of water.

"Bitch!" he cursed. "I'm going to carve you up like a damned turkey!"

He poured water, then dunked his face in the basin and blinked his eyes several times before he pulled his face up and dried it with his sleeve. Hagan stared at his reflection in the mirror. He cursed again because his vision was still a little blurry.

He bulled his way out of the bathroom and went over to the bed. He stared down at the unconscious woman and drew his knife, then decided that it would be no fun at all to cut a woman when she was knocked out cold. So he'd wait and do it after the chink returned. Maybe he'd even gag them both and cut them at the same time. He'd castrate the chink, then work on Rose.

Hagan liked that idea. He liked it so much that he sleeved his weeping eyes and went over to the window where he could oversee the street. He'd wait and watch for the chink, if his damned eyes ever cleared up. Then, when the man returned, he'd have his carving-up party.

Ki had left the Baron Hotel in order to meditate and exercise in a deep arroyo just south of town where he would not be observed. After limbering up, he'd spent an intense and vigorous hour practicing his kicks and hand strikes while wearing his familiar black ninja costume and sandals. Another half hour had passed quickly during meditation, and then he'd changed back into the uncomfortable suit, combed his hair neatly, and tied on the shoes he so hated. When his tie was once again pulled up close around his throat like a hangman's noose, he reluctantly walked back to town.

Tomorrow was Friday, and he knew that with each passing day, the danger increased. He had thought much about when an attack from Joe Hagan might take place, and he was convinced that the Arizona Strangler would not wait until he was on the stage, because it would be manned by extra guards. Hagan would be wary about trying to kill everyone including the driver. So, if Ki's reasoning was correct, and the banker and the editor really were part of the murderous plot that had claimed the lives of several good Arizonians, then Joe Hagan's attack would have to come within the next eighteen hours.

As Ki walked back into Tucson, he watched everything. The attacker might be wise enough to simply ambush him with a rifle. In that case, Ki knew that he had to keep his eyes constantly moving, especially upward toward rooftops and second-story windows.

He also moved as far out from the alley openings as he could without being conspicuous. But no attack came, and it was not until he looked up at his own room that he saw the outline of a very, very big man. The samurai's eyes flicked downward and he continued toward the hotel as if nothing had happened. To anyone who passed, he simply looked preoccupied.

And he was.

The samurai was also very angry that he'd left Rose alone. Sure, he'd told her not to open the door unless she was certain that it was safe. But he'd known that Rose was naive and far too trusting. So she'd been duped and now Joe Hagan was upstairs and waiting to make his kill.

The samurai considered Rose's welfare. She would

139

either be dead, or unconscious, or perhaps bound and gagged. Rose would never hold still while he walked unsuspectingly into a death trap.

Dammit! Ki thought, what I would give for my *han-kei*!

But at least he had his *shuriken* blades and his *tanto* blade. A blade that he knew would not stand up against the force of a Bowie knife but which was faster. And in knife fighting, speed, quickness, and outright agility plus unfailing courage were the ingredients that counted.

Ki entered the lobby of the hotel, and the desk clerk called a greeting to him that he acknowledged. He was something of a celebrity now that everyone in Tucson knew how he had thwarted the plans of the town banker and editor to make a financial killing. Ki had not seen either man since he'd left the bank, but he imagined they were being besieged with furious depositors demanding their money be returned. It gave the samurai a good feeling to know that, no matter what the outcome upstairs or in a court of law, John Miller and Hilton Turner were ruined and permanently disgraced.

Ki took the stairs two at a time and when he reached the upstairs landing, he looked both ways and then he quickly began to tear off his suit, shirt, tie, and leather shoes. Yes, he stood the chance that someone would exit their room and make some loud remark but it was worth the risk as he hurled his suit to the floor and quickly pulled on his own black and loose-fitting samurai outfit. He made sure his knife and the shuriken star blades were ready as he knocked on his own door.

There was no answer inside. Ki continued to hammer at the door. Finally, a deep voice just inches away growled, "Who is it?"

"Room service," Ki said, stepping back as far as he could into the shadows.

The bolt turned and when the knob turned as well, Ki jumped up and delivered a powerful flat-foot kick to the door. His bare foot punched through the wood and the door was knocked open, it's hinges sprung loose.

Ki landed badly because his bare foot caught in the jagged hole and he fell on his side. The door was torn open and Joe Hagan, still blurry-eyed, did not see Ki at his feet and tripped over him. He staggered forward and slammed into the opposite wall, then bounced back and jumped at Ki.

The samurai tore his foot out of the door and rolled as Hagan's dreaded Bowie knife bit into the hall carpet. Ki sprang to his feet and kicked again; this time his foot caught Hagan on the side of the face and knocked him back. Hagan was not even stunned, however. He cursed, yanked the tip of his huge knife from the floor, and lunged at his enemy.

Ki ducked and just managed to deliver a *migi-shoti* blow to Hagan's shoulder. It should have broken bone, but Hagan's strength was nearly inhuman and the samurai's hand bounced off without doing any noticeable damage.

The samurai glanced sideways at Rose. He saw blood on her face and wondered if she were dead or alive. He didn't have time to find out as Hagan slammed the broken door closed behind himself, raised his knife cutting edge up, and snarled, "Who the hell are you!"

Ki replied, "I intended to ask you the same question. Are you the Arizona Strangler?"

In response, Hagan threw his head back and laughed. "You ain't no goddamn chink. I never saw a Chinaman could put his foot through a solid wood door and then almost break my damn shoulder."

"Are you the strangler?" Ki repeated quietly as Hagan began to flick his knife back and forth.

"Yeah, I've strangled a few," Hagan said. "But

I'd rather cut a man to ribbons than use a wire or rope around his throat until his face turns purple and his tongue is stickin' out of his mouth big as a pickle.''

Ki drew his own *tanto* blade, and the sight of its slim steel made Hagan laugh with contempt. "Shit, man! I wouldn't use that bitty little sonofabitch to clean meat out from between my teeth!''

"You're here on orders from Miller and Turner, aren't you?" Ki asked.

"Damn right.''

"That's all I need to know. Now, come and get it," Ki said, crouching and starting to move to his left.

Hagan had learned a thing or two, and despite his big talk, he knew full well that the long, thin *tanto* blade could reach his heart or any one of his vital organs. It could slice the artery in his neck or his arm, and he'd lose consciousness in less than twenty seconds. Hagan knew all these things because he had killed a lot of Mexicans who'd considered themselves very good with a knife. And those that had watched in awe had given him his famed south-of-the-border nickname, El Cuchillo Grande.

"You come and get it," he said, moving his blade back and forth. "And how do you like what I done to your woman—my stupid, trusting wife?''

"Is she dead?" Ki feinted with his blade, but the big killer did not go for it and was not fooled in the least.

"Not yet. I want to screw her a few times before I carve her up. And I want her to watch you die.''

The Bowie knife swept in very fast and low. Ki jumped back, but Hagan's arms were so long that the knife still sliced his pants. "You're very, very good with that big steel," Ki said.

"I'm the best that ever lived after Jim Bowie. And if he'd have been around, I'd have challenged him to a fight to the death and gutted him like a deer.''

Again, Hagan's knife swept in and this time, Ki's own blade flicked out and sought the artery that ran down his forearm. He missed the artery, but Hagan's sleeve darkened wetly with blood.

"You're a quick yellow bastard," Hagan said. "I'll give you that much."

"How many men did you strangle for John Miller and Hilton Turner?" Ki asked, waiting for the lunge that he knew was about to come.

"That's for you to guess," Hagan said, feinting again with his knife, then kicking out with his long leg at Ki's knee. The samurai just managed to get back, and the moment that Hagan was off balance, Ki swept in with his tanto blade. He wanted Hagan alive so that the man could be made to talk and testify against Miller and Turner, so his knife did not seek a vital organ but instead the tendon in Hagan's left arm.

The tanto blade found the tendon and Hagan groaned. His left arm fell uselessly at his side, but his wicked Bowie scored, too, and Ki was staggered and his side was opened to the bone. Even so, they both understood that Hagan was now the one most seriously disadvantaged.

For the first time the leer of contempt was missing from Joe Hagan's handsome but cruel face. "Where'd you learn knife fighting like this?" he grunted, his powerful left arm swinging at his side like a string of sausages.

"In Japan," Ki said, feeling the blood leaking down into his trousers. "And you?"

"In Old Mexico," Hagan said. "You'll have to kill me on my feet to win."

"Then so be it," Ki said.

Hagan attacked in a rush. His knife seemed to be everywhere, and Ki retreated, his own blade unable to withstand the force of the heavier weapon. In vain, the samurai sought another opening. An opening he had decided to use for the kill because, even one-armed, Hagan was simply too strong and too skilled to risk trying to wound again. Ki had tried that once, and now his own side was laid open.

Ki stood before the window and felt a warm breeze on his back. Hagan closed in on him and their blades sang a deadly duel but the tanto was not the Bowie's equal in weight, and Ki, in a desperate move, ducked and tried to drive his steel into the exposed underbelly of the giant.

Hagan was coming forward and, with his incredibly quick reflexes, just managed to parry Ki's deadly thrust toward his mid-section. But in so doing, Joe Hagan lost his balance and crashed through the window.

Ki staggered, whirled, and looked down to see the huge man crash down on the slanted porch of the Baron Hotel and then roll off it into the street below. Joe Hagan, covered with blood and glass, came unsteadily to his feet as pedestrians fell back in shock and fear. Bowie knife still clutched in his big fist, Hagan swore at everyone and ran north up the street.

Ki went after him. He did not dare to stop and see if Rose was still alive. He *had* to catch Joe Hagan. If the man escaped, everything was lost.

When the samurai raced down the stairs and across the lobby, no one recognized him as the cultured Mr. Ki. What they saw was a bloodied demon with a thin knife in his hand.

Ki slammed into a pedestrian that was entering the hotel and knocked the man clear out into the street as he turned and raced in the direction Joe Hagan had taken.

"Where'd he go?" Ki shouted a block later when he'd lost sight of the strangler.

A wide-eyed boy no older than ten pointed at a barn near the edge of Tucson. Ki ran on.

When he came to the big double doors of the barn, Ki found a man lying in a pool of his own blood, and Ki figured it must have been the unfortunate owner of the stable who had tried to stop Joe Hagan.

The samurai pulled a shuriken blade out of his tunic and dropped to his knees, shifting his tanto blade into his left hand before he edged around the door.

Hagan was waiting for him on the other side of the door. With a roar, he jumped on Ki's back, looped his powerful right arm around Ki's throat, and then lifted him completely off the dirt floor. Hagan wrenched at Ki like a wolf would a bone he was tearing from a carcass. Ki felt his neck snap and knew that it could not take another violent movement like that. He'd die of a broken neck before he was strangled.

The samurai twisted the tanto blade backward and drove it blindly up into Joe Hagan's flat stomach. He felt the man grunt, and Ki pulled the blade out and drove it in once more.

Hagan screamed and tried to break Ki's neck, but already his enormous strength was draining from his good right arm and the tanto blade kept ripping up into his vitals.

Hagan dropped to his knees, still struggling to break the samurai's neck as the life in him flickered and then died.

Ki, choking and unable to move his neck, collapsed and then lay still until he lost consciousness.

When he awoke, Rose was at his bedside and her face was swollen all lopsided, but she was still smiling. "It's over," she whispered. "He's dead."

Ki nodded. "I wanted his confession for the mur-

145

der of Warren Hastings and the conviction of John Miller and Hilton Turner.''

Rose said, ''They're ruined. They've been arrested for fraud and I expect them to go to prison. That's worse than a death sentence for two prideful men like that. Besides, Joe was the one that had to be killed.''

Rose touched his face. ''The doctor said you've lost a great deal of blood and your neck has been injured.''

Ki tried to turn his head. A sharp and instant pain filled his head, and he knew fear. If he were paralyzed . . .

''The doctor said that the pain and paralysis will go away after a few weeks, a month at the most. He examined your neck and you have no paralysis in your feet or hands.'' Rose leaned forward and kissed his cheek. ''You're going to be fine. It will just take time.''

Ki nodded. With the Arizona Strangler dead, Jessie's life was no longer in danger. So unless there were other men who also were stranglers, Ki knew he could afford to rest and recover.

But two days later Mrs. Hale came to see Ki. She sat down beside his bed and said, ''Mr. Ki, first I want to thank you for bringing to justice the man that killed my late husband. I knew it was Joe Hagan all along, even though poor Ralph was hung by mistake. And guess what?''

Since Ki could not even move his neck, he waited. The widow drew out her late husband's ring which she had sketched for Jessie. It was a perfect match with its five diamonds. ''I guess this leaves little doubt in anyone's mind that Joe Hagan killed my husband, damn his eyes!''

Mrs. Hale dabbed a silk kerchief at her own eyes. ''And it seems that Hagan did not trust anyone. Back in the cave where the sheriff found that poor

Apache slave, there were records that tie both John Miller and Hilton Turner into the killing.''

Good, Ki thought.

"They'll go to prison for life," Mrs. Hale said, her voice shaking with anger. "But I'm afraid that all of this strangling business isn't yet over."

Ki blinked. "What do you mean?"

"I mean that there were also some other names found in that cave. Names that leave little doubt that Hagan, Miller and Turner were working with some people in Yuma."

Ki felt a chill pass down his spine. "Their names!"

"Arnold Beard. Oscar Montoya. Art Logman and Jess Whitlow." Mrs. Hale frowned. "But isn't he the sheriff of Yuma?"

"Yes," Ki said tightly. And both Logman and Montoya are locked in the Yuma Prison!"

"That's impossible," Mrs. Hale said.

"Why?"

"Because Joe Hagan's notes made it very clear that Montoya and Logman had also strangled for pay."

The samurai tried to sit up but the pain in his neck was so terrible he knew that he risked injuring himself permanently. If that happened, he would be of no use to Jessie at all. "We have to get word to Miss Starbuck at once," he said.

"I'm afraid that is also impossible," Mrs. Hale said. "In fact, when the sheriff found those names and this ring, the first thing I attempted to do was to telegraph Miss Starbuck and warn her of her danger. But the telegraph wires are down, and because of the Apache, nothing is moving between here and Yuma."

The samurai groaned. "There must be something we can do!"

"Yes, there is." Dear Mrs. Hale patted the samurai on the forehead. "We must pray for her."

And before Ki could say a word, the lady bowed

her head and began to pray. Ki appreciated that, but somehow, he wanted to do more and yet . . . yet for the very first time in his life, he was absolutely helpless.

★

Chapter 13

Jessica Starbuck was troubled, and as she sat at her desk, she kept rewriting four names. Art Logman. Oscar Montoya. Arnold Beard, and Jess Whitlow, the sheriff of Yuma.

"We've *got* to do something to force their hand," Jessie said to Cassandra Hastings. "We aren't getting anywhere waiting for them to come at us."

"But what if the list is wrong?" Cassandra said. "I mean, yes, it was written by my husband. But it could have been just a list of suspects, maybe only one of which is the Arizona Strangler."

"Maybe," Jessie said. "But I don't think we can assume anything but that all four men are somehow involved."

"How would Montoya and Logman be involved? They're in prison."

"Are they?" Jessie asked. "That's something that I've been told, but what if they're not?"

"I don't understand," Cassandra said. "They were sentenced to life without parole."

"Then I'm going to make sure that they're serving it out," Jessie said. "I'm going to pay them a visit."

"They won't let a woman in there!"

Jessie's brow furrowed. "All right, then I guess that I'll have to ask Lieutenant Jason Caldwell. He's a doctor and I'm sure he can think of some ruse to pay a visit to those two prisoners."

With that decision made, Jessie sent for the doctor. Lieutenant Caldwell grabbed his medical bag just in case and left his infirmary at Fort Yuma and came at once. When he reached the Hastings house and was invited inside, he was smiling. "What a lucky fellow I am to enjoy the company of the two most beautiful women in the entire Arizona Territory and perhaps . . . perhaps even the entire West."

Cassandra blushed. She had begun to notice the opposite sex again, and if Jessie had not already captured the young army doctor's heart, she might even have been interested. But with Jessie firmly in the forefront, Cassandra remained very guarded about her own romantic needs. Besides, she felt a little guilty that she was already starting to notice a handsome young man while her dear husband was barely two months gone.

"Cassandra, your cheeks are becoming rosy," the lieutenant said. "Surely it is not because of my compliment."

Jessie watched the couple thinking that, after she was gone, this might be a wonderful match. But for now, there was a mystery to solve and little time for matters of the heart. "Jason, I need you to check on two inmates at the prison."

The army doctor's smile faded. "I'm afraid that's out of my jurisdiction," he said. "In fact, I've offered my services there, and the warden has made no bones about telling me that I should stick to the fort and my own business.''

"But what if an inmate becomes sick or is stabbed in a fight? Don't those things sometimes happen?''

"Quite often,'' the army doctor admitted. "But the attitude by the warden seems to be that, if an inmate dies, then so what? The Arizona Territory reaps a savings.''

"How callous!'' Cassandra exclaimed.

"Perhaps so,'' Jessie said. "But I suspect that attitude concerning inmates also exists in almost every state and territory in the Union. Jason, I still need you to go into that prison and find out if two inmates are actually incarcerated as they are supposed to be.''

"You want to know if Art Logman and Oscar Montoya are there, or if they've flown the coop. Is that it?''

"Exactly,'' Jessie said. "As it is now, all we know is that they are *supposed* to be in that prison. You have to find out.''

"I'll do it this afternoon,'' Jason said, "and all I ask in repayment is that I be allowed to take you out to dinner and perhaps a nice after-dinner walk along the Colorado River.''

When the doctor winked, Jessie almost laughed aloud. The man had no intentions of "walking'' her any distance. What he meant was that he very badly wanted to make love with her again in the cool river water.

"All right,'' she said. "It's a deal. Only I insist on buying the dinner, and I think that I should like to invite Cassandra along.''

"Oh, no!'' Cassandra said quickly. "I really don't want to intrude.''

"It won't be an intrusion,'' Jason said, forcing gallantry. "I also insist that you join us.''

Cassandra could not hide her pleasure at the invi-

151

tation. She had not been out to dinner since before her husband had been murdered. "Then I accept," she told them.

Jason left only a few minutes later, saying, "I will be by to escort you ladies at eight o'clock. By then, I intend to have actually seen both prisoners."

"Have you any idea how you're going to accomplish this feat?"

"No," the doctor admitted. "But by the time I reach the prison, I will surely have thought of some clever ruse."

As the doctor walked briskly away, Cassandra said. "He is such a dynamic man. Obviously well bred, too."

"Obviously," Jessie said.

Jason looked back and waved at the two women, and then he continued on toward the prison, his mind churning at the problem of how he was going to talk his way past the guards and the warden. He had never been inside the prison, and despite its reputation as being a hard place, Dr. Caldwell had always been curious. Now he needed to come up with a clever idea.

Five minutes later he was standing at the gate and speaking to a prison guard who held a sawed-off shotgun as if it were an extension of his arm. "I must see the warden," Jason insisted. "It is a matter of life and death."

"Whose life and death?"

Jason looked the man squarely in the eye. "Perhaps your own. There are reports of smallpox in this community, and I've already treated several soldiers at the fort. If that disease spreads in this prison, you'll get it just as quick as an inmate. You ever seen anyone die of smallpox?"

The guard nodded his head up and down. "Damn right I have! It was terrible."

"Then take me to your warden at once," Jason

152

demanded with impatience. "I may be your only hope."

The guard let him inside and they hurried to the warden's office. The warden's name was Horace Hammond, and though Jason had seen him many times on the streets of Yuma, they had never spoken. Hammond was a short, fat man who sweated as profusely as he cussed.

"What the hell is an army doctor doin' in my prison!" he snapped the moment that Jason entered his filthy little office. "I told you this was off-bounds for soldiers. Guard, what the hell you let him in here for!"

"Warden, he's got something real important to say."

"It better be important. Speak your piece, Lieutenant. I got work to do and no time for the army."

"What did the army ever do to you?" Jason asked on an impulsive hunch. "Were you drummed out or what?"

"That's none of your damned concern! Now, what is it you're here for?"

"There's a very real chance that we are about to have an outbreak of smallpox," Jason said without wasting any time on preliminaries.

"Smallpox!"

Jason was delighted to see that the very mention of the dreaded disease brought the warden straight out of his chair. "That's right. And I need to observe every inmate in this prison."

The warden closed his mouth, opened it, then closed it again and swallowed. "Sonofabitch! Smallpox? I hear there's a medicine for it now?"

"It's an experimental medicine," Jason said, patting his medical bag and deciding that he would just have to use the large number of aspirin powders that he carried as a cure-all for everything from back

153

strain to hangovers. "I have medicinal powders that could save your lives."

"Well, give me one of the damned things right now!" the warden demanded.

Jason opened his bag and gave one to the warden and another to the guard. "How many other guards and other personnel do you have on your staff?"

"Eight."

Jason dispensed eight additional powders. The warden took a bottle of whiskey from his desk drawer, then poured himself two fingers and added the powder before drinking it down straight. The guard left in a rush without asking permission.

"Now," Jason said, "shall we get right to it? I don't need to touch the prisoners, I just need their names, ages, and general health status?"

"Health status?" The warden snorted with derision. "Hell, they're all healthy as horses. Personally, I wouldn't mind it a damn bit if smallpox wiped the buggers out to a man. Save the taxpayers money and save me the headache of watchin' 'em all the damned time."

"If that happened," Jason said, "you'd be out of a job. And frankly, I don't see you in the role of a banker or merchant."

Hammond grunted, burped whiskey, and aspirin fumes, then wagged his head up and down in agreement. "Yeah," he said, "I suppose you've got a point. This is where I belong. But these men are animals. They're cold-blooded killers."

Jason did not want to spend a moment longer than was necessary with this man in his filthy office. "Can we get started?"

The warden pushed his bulk around his office desk and led the way outside. They passed through another gate and then entered a stark compound where the prisoners were kept in rock cells that the doctor would not have wished upon a dog.

"My God!" he whispered. "This is inhumane."

"There's nothing human about inmates," the warden said, coming up to the first prison cell and yelling, "Hackman!"

From inside the dirty cell a man turned and stared at the warden who growled, "You feelin' okay?"

"Hell, yes," Hackman growled. "I'm gonna live long enough to get paroled, and then I'm coming back here and put my knife in your fat guts!"

Jason swallowed nervously. He stepped closer and said, "I'm an army doctor. Have you experienced any sudden chills or fever? Any dizziness or diarrhea?"

"You mean the runs?"

"Yes."

"No," Hackman hissed. "And if I did I wouldn't tell you."

"Take one of these," Jason said, holding out one of the aspirin powders. "You'll feel better."

"You can shove that up your ass, Doctor!"

Jason dropped the powder back into his medical bag. He knew the entire inmate population was within hearing and not a word of their conversation was missed. "Suit yourself. If you want to die very miserably of smallpox, that's your decision."

"Smallpox!"

"That's right. As you may or may not know, it can be fatal, and even if you live it will scar you horribly."

The filthy inmate rushed to the cell door so suddenly that Jason leapt back, thinking that he was being attacked.

"Give me that medicine!"

Jason did as he was asked, and then he moved on to the next patient, and the next and the next. In each case, he demanded that the warden give him the inmate's name and his age.

It was not until he was almost through and came

to the very last pair of cells near the east wall of the prison that the warden barked, "Montoya!"

Jason blinked at the man. He was smallish, but quite powerful, and he looked to be in his late twenties. He was obviously half Mexican and half white.

"Montoya," Jason said. "Your first name and age."

"Oscar, age twenty-five." Montoya took the medicine. "What's this smallpox business? I never . . ."

"Montoya!" the warden snapped. "You know that prisoners are forbidden to ask questions. You just answer them, is that understood?"

Montoya's lip curled, but he took his powder and went back to the rear of his cell without saying another word.

"Logman," the warden said, "you're the last. Come up and take your medicine."

Logman was the same height as the doctor and probably about the same age. But that was all they had in common. Logman's face was already pitted and he said, "I had smallpox when I was a boy. Can't you tell?"

"Yes," Jason said, looking into the man's cold, pitiless eyes. "But you'd better take this anyway. A second bout could finish you off. What is your age?"

"Thirty-one. What's yours?"

"The same."

Their eyes locked and Jason felt an involuntary shiver pass up and down his spine. Logman snorted with derision. "You look like a prissy sonofabitch to me, Doc. I'll bet you wouldn't last a week in this cell before you'd go crazy."

Jason stepped back. "I'd last," he said. "But I'm too smart to ever wind up living like an animal."

Logman's eyes radiated pure hatred. "You bastards always got things the easy way. You're supposed to be an officer and a gentleman, but you're no different than any man in this hell hole. You just was born with the right set of parents and a silver spoon in your mouth. You had all the breaks and we had none of them.''

''What are you in here for?''

''Murder,'' Logman said. ''I strangled a rich sonofabitch like you when he tried to spark my girlfriend.''

''Logman!'' the warden snapped. ''That's enough!''

The prisoner stuck his big hand through the bars, and Jason gave him a packet of medicine, then turned and walked toward the gate.

''Hey!''

Jason stopped and turned to see the warden come puffing up to him.

''What about this epidemic? Are you coming back tomorrow with more medicine?''

''No,'' Jason said, pulling his troubled thoughts from what he had just seen and heard. ''Not unless one of your men comes down with the pox. In that case, contact me at once.''

''Maybe you should quarantine this place.''

''Won't be necessary,'' Jason said, continuing toward the gate that would deliver him from this stinking hell hole. ''Just keep an eye out for sickness, and if it comes, you know where I'll be.''

''How about a couple extra packets for me?'' the warden said, hurrying along beside him. ''I mean, if one is good, two or three might be even better. Isn't that right?''

''No, it isn't,'' Jason said.

The warden stopped and watched him leave. As soon as Jason hurried out through the prison gates, he felt an immediate sense of light-headedness. He took a deep breath of free air and did not look back as he headed to Fort Yuma. Tonight, he would tell

157

Jessie and Cassandra that the two prisoners on Warren Hastings's list of suspects should be scratched.

Art Logman and Oscar Montoya were both in Yuma Prison just as they were supposed to be. No doubt either man had the killer instincts to hire out as stranglers. But you could not do that from behind bars.

★

Chapter 14

Jessie and Jason stepped into the mortician's parlor and studied the face of the dead Yuma banker. The man had been laid out in a silk-lined coffin, and although his face was powdered, nothing could hide the bluish cast to his skin and the fixed expression of terror that had claimed his features at the moment of his hideous death.

The lieutenant shook his head. "I banked with him, but I never much cared for the man. He was pretty stuffy. But to die that way . . . well, even murderers break their necks in a hangman's noose and go swiftly."

When Jessie said nothing, the doctor unbuttoned the man's collar and removed his tie before he examined the banker's badly bruised neck. "Hmmmm," he grunted with interest.

"Hmmmm what?" Jessie asked impatiently.

"Oh, sorry. I was just noticing that Mr. Fields

159

was strangled by the same means as was your late friend, Warren Hastings. Whoever did this was a powerful man, and he used a length of either cord or thin rope.''

"That doesn't tell us much.''

"No,'' Jason said, stepping back from the corpse and shaking his head. "It doesn't tell us much of anything.''

Jessie averted her eyes from the dead man and said, "What I need to do is find a link between this man and the names of suspects left to us by Warren.''

"That's true,'' the doctor said, taking her outside and escorting her down the boardwalk. "But now that we've eliminated Art Logman and Oscar Montoya from the list, we have only our sheriff and Mr. Arnold Beard.''

"That's right,'' Jessie said. "I'm going to pay Mr. Beard a visit this afternoon on the pretext of needing some legal advice. Perhaps I can win his confidence.''

The doctor chuckled. "With your looks, you can win anything you want from Beard. He considers himself to be quite a ladies' man. I'll bet he propositions you within the first hour.''

"He can proposition me all day long,'' Jessie said, "if I feel that I'm getting closer to finding out the truth behind these terrible stranglings.''

"I understand that Cassandra was pretty upset about this.''

"That's right,'' Jessie said. "And you'll have to tell her that it's highly likely that, whoever killed her husband also killed Mr. Fields.''

"I can give her a sedative,'' Jason said. "What are we going to do about Sheriff Whitlow? His name was on the list, too.''

"One thing at a time,'' Jessie said. "After I pay a visit to Mr. Beard, then I'll stop by the sheriff's office and put some pressure on him to make an arrest for this latest murder."

The lieutenant stopped and said, "You're pushing these people to the wall. Do you know that?"

"What choice do I have? If I do nothing, someone else is going to die. I've been expecting Ki to return, but he's still gone and I'm worried about him. I'd give anything to know what he's found out in Tucson. But because of the Apache, nothing is getting across the Sonora Desert."

"Your samurai would want you to play it safe, at least until he returns," Jason said. "Why don't you and Cassandra just sit tight until then?"

"I'm not made that way," Jessie said. She patted the young army doctor's cheek. "Now, why don't you go along and keep Cassandra company while I see if I can trap Mr. Beard."

"He's damned clever," Jason said. "I've heard that again and again. But his weakness is his vanity. Everyone who's ever dealt with the man will tell you that he is a sucker for flattery."

"Thanks," Jessie said. "I'll remember that."

When Jessie met Arnold Beard in his plush attorney's office, it was immediately apparent that Jason had been correct about the man's enormous vanity. Beard had even commissioned a portrait of himself standing in front of both an American flag and one that symbolized the long awaited State of Arizona.

Beard was her own age, and although he was of only average height, he was blond, good looking in a roguish sort of way, and looked very fit. "Ahh, Miss Starbuck!" he exclaimed, smiling with perfect white teeth and a politician's smile. "What an honor it is to have you visit my humble office."

"Nothing humble about it," Jessie said, turning her own brilliant smile. "It is a magnificent office. That cabinet is French, fourteenth century, I'd say."

161

Beard's eyes lit up. "Well, you *are* impressive. Yes, it is, and my desk was carved by a Spanish monk in the sixteenth century. The vase over there is Dutch, and it's priceless. The painting of the horses and carriage you no doubt admire on the west wall is also priceless even though it is unsigned. Personally, I believe it very likely that the artist was none other than Renoir. Wouldn't you agree?"

Jessie knew that she had to agree and there was no point in stating that an unsigned painting, no matter how good it might be, was hardly priceless. "Oh, yes," Jessie said. "I see a great deal of Renoir's genius in the colors and the bold strokes."

Beard was delighted that she agreed. "Please," he said, eyeing her with a mixture of admiration and outright lust. "Have a seat. Can I offer you something to drink? Cognac? Wine? Champagne? I feel that your visit is most certainly an excuse for a small celebration."

"I'd rather not have anything to drink, but by all means have something yourself."

Beard went to an antique liquor cabinet that must have cost him thousands of dollars and poured a glass of French cognac from a crystal decanter. He turned, showed his perfect teeth, and said, "I have heard many stories about your father and the famed Starbuck Enterprises. I understand that even though you have worldwide holdings, you much prefer the life of a Texas cattle rancher."

"That's right."

"How quaint." He sipped his drink and added, "One would expect a woman of your beauty, intelligence, and class to live in the East or in Europe, where there is real culture. But not on the Texas frontier. It doesn't seem to fit you."

Jessie's smile did not slip although she felt like telling this man that he had no idea what "fit" her. "Well," she said, "in the quiet depths of our soul,

162

we are all fathomless mysteries to one another, and so that is the wonder of humanity, its infinite and unlikely diversities.''

"Ohh, I like that! Aristotle?"

"Alex Starbuck," she said, watching his face color with embarrassment.

Arnold Beard was not accustomed to being wrong or made light of by anyone. He cleared his throat and tried a little harder to ingratiate himself with this rich and beautiful young woman. The most desirable woman he'd ever seen. And as his eyes slipped to the large swell of her breasts, he felt his root stir inside his trousers with anticipation. If he could bed this bronze-haired beauty, my God, what . . .

"Mr. Beard," Jessie said, feeling her own cheeks warm under the heat of his eyes. "I contacted you because I am unable to contact my own attorneys. And a woman of means without legal council can be very vulnerable indeed."

"Indeed!" he said, pulling his mind sharply back to business. Beard knew that he had to impress this woman intellectually before physically. He also knew what most of Tucson suspected—that Jessie was having an affair with the young army doctor, Lieutenant Caldwell. "Now, how can I service you . . . I mean *serve* you best?"

"I need to know a little about the laws of this territory."

"All right. What kinds of laws?"

"Let's take capital punishment," Jessie said, watching his face and seeing his surprise. "You see, my dear friend Warren Hastings was strangled to death and the culprit remains a free man. Now, if he was apprehended and brought to trial, then convicted of murder, would this territory suffer any liability to his widow because Warren's murder was the result of his public employment as a prosecutor?"

Arnold Beard had not expected anything like this

sort of question. "Well," he said, "I think perhaps a court of law might find some culpability on the part of the territory. But it would all depend upon the evidence presented. Certainly, any public official—especially a prosecuting attorney who is directly responsible for sentencing men to death and to prison—must realize that he assumes risk when he seeks office, be it elected or appointed."

"Have you ever thought of seeking office?" Jessie asked. "I mean, you make a very presentable figure, and I'm sure you would prove quite electable."

"Do you think so? Oh, that is nice of you to say. And actually, I think I will seek public office some day. Perhaps when the territory achieves statehood."

"Yes," Jessie said, "I saw that portrait of you, and I thought it very likely that you might."

"Do you like it?"

"Very much. Of course, it doesn't nearly do you justice." That was not true. The portrait was extremely flattering.

"Well, now!" Beard said, puffing up to his full five feet ten inches and then coming around to take Jessie by the hands and stare longingly into her eyes. "You do give me a great compliment. Are you sure you won't have a drink with me?"

"Perhaps tonight."

"Wonderful. I'll be by at eight. I think we'll have a great deal to talk about."

"I'm sure we will," Jessie said sweetly.

Jessie left him shortly after that and went to see the sheriff. Jess Whitlow was reading a newspaper when she walked inside. When he saw her, the sheriff stood up and said, "Well, if it isn't Miss Jessica Starbuck. What brings you back here? Have you found out who Warren's killer was yet, or do you still think that I'm one of the prime suspects because my name is on his list?"

"What I think is that you had better apprehend the

164

Arizona Strangler before he kills anyone else. Do you have any suspects for the murder of Mr. Fields?"

The sheriff blustered. "There's an investigation taking place," he said. "But I don't see that it's any of your damned business."

"It's everyone's business when a sheriff doesn't do his job."

Whitlow's eyes blazed with anger. "Some people should mind their own damned business," he said.

"I'm going to find out who killed your banker and my friend," Jessie said. "Just as soon as the stage begins to come through Yuma again, I'm going to send for a few hand-picked investigators. They're tough and they know how to get answers. I think you already know those answers, and that your name wasn't on Warren Hastings's list without a good reason. If I were you, Sheriff, I'd think about having a long talk with an attorney."

"You're damn crazy!"

Jessie did not step back even though she thought that the sheriff was past the point of reason. "We'll see. As soon as the telegraph lines are back in operation and the stages are running, we'll just see. One of the first orders of business for my investigators will be to check your background so thoroughly that they'll know everything about your past. Everything."

Now Jessie did step back to the door and open it because Sheriff Jess Whitlow was shaking with fury. Jessie backed into the street. "I hope you don't have anything to hide, Sheriff. I hope there are no skeletons in your closet."

Whitlow cursed and charged the door. Jessie heard it slam as she hurried down the boardwalk. Well, she thought, if that didn't push him into some kind of rash action, nothing I could ever say would.

Jessie stepped into a milliner's shop and stayed near the front window, pretending to browse but

165

actually keeping her eye on the sheriff's office. A few minutes later she was rewarded with the sight of Jess Whitlow hurrying outside.

Jessie waited a few moments, then followed him. Yuma was not a big town and it took her only one block to realize that Sheriff Whitlow was on his way to Arnold Beard's law office.

Jessie cut down the back alley behind the law office and moved as quickly as she could until she reached the side of the office. Easing forward, knowing that she was risking a great deal to do this in broad daylight when anyone might come along and see her, Jessie felt she really had little choice but to take the chance that had been presented.

She stopped just below the attorney's window and stood very still. It wasn't hard to hear the conversation because both men were angry.

"I tell you," Whitlow said, "that woman is going to bring investigators into this town when the Apache threat is over, and she is going to blow everything up in our faces. Every damn thing!"

"Nonsense! She hasn't a clue."

"She has a list with my name on it! Maybe with your name on it as well. Hastings was no fool. He could see what was going on and that's why he had to be killed before he ruined everything."

"Hastings is dead. Any list he wrote is meaningless in a court of law."

"The hell with a court of law!" Whitlow shouted. "If Starbuck gets people into Yuma and they ask enough questions and offer enough money to someone who will answer those questions, we'd have to have a dozen people killed to protect ourselves."

"We'll do whatever we have to do. Fields was a fool to siphon off funds and send them to Tucson to finance the purchase of more real estate. And when that damn samurai tricked them all . . . well, it's finished for us there. But we can still achieve our

166

purposes if we don't lose our heads. With Fields dead, there's no longer a link between us, John Miller, and Hilton Turner.''

"Oh, yeah, why not?"

"Because as soon as we can send our two boys over there, another banker and Tucson's editor are the same as dead.''

The sheriff's voice softened. "Good," he said. "But while the boys are still here, I think they'd better strangle Cassandra Hastings and that damned Starbuck woman.''

"That is exactly what we don't want to happen,'' Beard argued. "If they were strangled, then the whole thing would attract national attention. Can you imagine the headlines that would cover all the newspapers proclaiming that two beautiful women, one rich and famous, were both strangled to death in Yuma? Why, reporters from all over the country would swarm in here the first chance, and they'd soon learn about our other stranglings and before we knew it, someone would be asking us some very hard questions.''

"Someone is going to ask them to us anyway if Starbuck isn't stopped.''

"You leave her to me," Beard said. "I'm taking her to dinner tonight. And then afterward, I'll take care of her. By tomorrow she'll be eating out of my hand.''

"I dunno," the sheriff said, his voice dubious. "I think you might just have met your match with this woman. She's smart and she's powerful. I say kill her and Cassandra Hastings and let's not take any chances.''

"No. Not until I at least have a chance to win her over.''

"Win her over to what!" the sheriff demanded. "All you want is what any man would want from her. And I'm telling you, it ain't worth going to the gallows to climb between those long legs of hers!''

"You're a crude man, Sheriff. Now, go away and I'll talk with you tomorrow. I think that . . .''

Jessie figured that she had heard all she needed to hear. She didn't yet know who the stranglers were, but now she knew that Arnold Beard and the sheriff of Yuma were up to their murderous necks in some plot that Warren Hastings had uncovered.

Jessie turned and started to hurry back down the alley, but suddenly a large wiry-haired dog came trotting around the corner of the attorney's office. When it saw her, the hair on its back lifted and a rumble filled its throat. Jessie froze. She knew better than to run, and yet she knew that she had to get away.

"Go on,'' she whispered.

The damn dog began to bark. Jessie saw a heavy stick and edged over to it, and when it was firmly in her grasp, she started toward the barking dog, knowing that it was going to bring someone out to investigate.

The big dog jumped toward her, stopped at the last instant and snapped viciously. Jessie wound up and hit it as hard as she could across the snout. The animal yelped with pain and Jessie hit it again and the dog reversed direction and took off running.

Jessie heard the sheriff's voice yell something and then she took off running as fast as her legs would carry her. She expected to hear a gunshot before she finally reached the end of the alley but the shot never came. Jessie dashed back onto the main street and walked quickly toward Cassandra Hastings's house. Had the sheriff seen and recognized her before she'd gotten out of that alley?

There was no telling. But Jessie was afraid that he might well have. And if he had . . . she pushed the thought out of her mind. Tonight at eight o'clock she had a dinner date with Arnold Beard, and she knew that he would never allow her to be killed until after he'd had at least one chance to bed her. But she'd refuse him, and then he'd be as ready to have her killed as the sheriff.

Yes, Jessie thought, I either sleep with him, or my life isn't worth a plug nickel starting tomorrow.

★

Chapter 15

Arnold Beard leaned across the table and spilled his champagne on the tablecloth. "How clumsy of me!" he said, snapping his fingers imperiously for a waiter to clean up his mess.

Jessie just smiled. The Yuma attorney had had too much champagne to drink, and yet she hoped he drank even more. What she wanted was to have the man lower his guard and give her some real evidence that she could use against him in court. But given that he was smart and knew the law, Jessie realized that getting the man to talk too much was a lot to expect.

The waiter mopped up the tablecloth and said, "Would you like to take another table, Mr. Beard?"

"Naw, this one is fine. Just lay a couple dry towels over that wet spot and bring us another bottle of French champagne. The lady is enjoying herself. Right, Jessica?"

He leered at her and it was all Jessie could do not to toss her glassful of champagne in his face. Instead, she forced a brittle smile and said, "Yes, Arnold. I'm having a wonderful time."

"Good." His smile faded into a look of concern, and he leaned forward and took Jessie's hands in his own. She knew better than to pull away from him.

"Jessie," he said, "I'm afraid we've got a little problem between us. It's one that we have to talk out."

Jessie feigned ignorance. "Why, whatever kind of problem are you talking about?"

"I think you know exactly what I'm talking about. It takes a pretty bright woman to run the kind of empire that your father built. From everything I've heard, you've even made it bigger and richer. So please, don't play dumb and beautiful with me. I know that you know that I know why you're here."

He grinned loosely. "Did that make any sense?"

"No," Jessie said, watching his face closely and feeling him squeeze her hands too tightly. The attorney's smile was frozen and it was a little unnerving.

"Let me explain more fully," he said. "You're here with me because my name is on that damned old list that Warren Hastings left in his safe. Now, isn't that the truth?"

"You're hurting me," Jessie said between clenched teeth. "Let go of my hands!"

He let go. "All right, now that I've done what you asked, answer my question. Am I on that list?"

Jessie decided that she had better tell this man the truth. "Yes, you are."

The news made him stiffen and blink, though he had expected it. "And you think that I might have something to do with all the stranglings. Is that also true?"

"The possibility has crossed my mind."

"And finally," he said, his voice hardening, "that

was you in the alley that the dog was snarling and barking at behind my office this afternoon. Isn't that also true?"

"No," she said, deciding that she could not dare to admit such a thing. If he were certain that it had been her who had eavesdropped, then he'd probably have tried to kill her by now. Jessie forced anger into her voice. "And I resent that accusation very much! I don't need to lower myself to that level. I can hire men to do my bidding."

His shoulders relaxed a little. "That's what I thought. But . . . well, never mind. What I need to know is how can I convince you that I'm innocent of any connection with the Arizona Strangler?"

Jessie had anticipated such a question. "You could discover his true identity and see that he is brought to justice," she said.

"You say him. Are you so sure that only one person is involved?"

It was Jessie's turn to be surprised by a question. "Actually, I just assumed that only one person could be so demented as to enjoy garroting his victims. The thought never occurred to me that there might be several such degenerates."

Beard smiled tolerantly. "You are rich, beautiful, and intelligent, but you're still a little naive. The Yuma Prison is full of such monsters. Most did not commit their murders out of passion, but out of greed. That prison and, indeed, the entire world is full of men who kill for money."

Jessie said nothing. The sad truth of the matter was that he was right.

Beard refilled his glass, tossed it down, and filled it again. "You're not keeping up with me," he said. "And I'm afraid you are hoping that I get completely drunk and hang myself with my own loose tongue."

Now Jessie did take a drink. "Arnold, let's not

172

pussyfoot around anymore," she said. "You know what I want and I know what you want."

His eyebrows lifted in mock surprise. "Oh, now we are finally going to be honest with each other? What do you think I really want?"

"To go to bed with me in the ridiculous hope that your lovemaking will win my heart and somehow my money."

"It could happen!"

"Not a chance."

He flushed with anger. "How can you be so sure? Is it because you're getting a nightly dose of that damned army doctor!"

Jessie slapped his face so hard that everyone in the room stopped eating and talking. "I'm leaving," she said. "And yes, you are correct when you say I want to nail your hide to the barn door. I think that you're up to your neck in murder."

"Shut up!" he choked. Then, lowering his voice, he hissed, "And you're right that I want you in bed. And I'm going to have you—tonight."

"You'll have me when hell freezes over."

Beard glanced toward the door and saw the sheriff. He nodded his head and the man disappeared before Jessie could turn around.

"Who was that you signaled to?" she asked.

"I'll ask you the questions," Beard said, his voice shaking with anger. "And the first question is—are you coming to bed with me, or is Cassandra Hastings going to be the next victim of the Arizona Strangler? It really could happen."

Jessie's heart dropped to her feet. "You wouldn't dare!"

"I have no say in the matter," he said, throwing his hands up and pretending innocence. "All I'm saying is that stranger things have happened. And I think, that if you don't fulfill my wishes, something

173

terrible might happen to her. Do you understand me?''

''Perfectly.''

Jessie wanted to claw his eyes out. And if she hadn't asked the lieutenant to watch over Cassandra, then she would have felt that all was lost. And maybe it was lost anyway. All she knew for certain this moment was that she would rather die than submit to this man's carnal desires. But she had to buy time. Had to make him think he had won.

''It seems,'' she whispered, ''that for perhaps the very first time I have been outsmarted. Congratulations.''

''Thank you,'' he said. ''But it will be a hollow victory for me if we can't be nice to each other. I mean, really nice. There's no need for us to be enemies.''

''There's not?''

''No. So why don't we finish this bottle of champagne and get better acquainted before I take you home and show you my pleasures?''

Jessie drank her champagne and held her glass out. ''Why don't we just stay here a little longer and then call it a night.''

He laughed. ''You try so hard to resist me. And it's all so foolish. When I make love to you, you'll see what you would have missed if I hadn't taken all the precautions necessary to have things go my way.''

When the sheriff left at Beard's signal, he made the decision that Cassandra Hastings and Jessica Starbuck both had to die. Beard was being played for a fool, but then, it had been Jess Whitlow's name that had been on the list of suspects, not the attorney's.

Whitlow hurried down the street to his saddled and waiting horse and then mounted it. He galloped across town, and when he came to the gates of Yuma Prison, he was allowed to enter without question. "Evenin', Sheriff. I'm afraid the Warden went to bed early."

"He'll get up for me," the sheriff said, trotting past the guard and then tying his horse up beside the warden's little rock house. It wasn't much of a house, but it was better than the cells that the prisoners had to live in. Hell, Whitlow thought, anything was better than being an inmate in this stinking prison.

Whitlow didn't even bother to knock but went right inside. He struck a match on the doorframe and when he used it to guide his way to a kerosene lantern, he lit the lamp and held it aloft over the warden's face.

"Damn you, Sheriff! What the hell are you doing here at this time of night!"

"We got a job for Logman and Montoya," the sheriff said.

"Well, can't it wait?" the warden cried, holding his hand over his eyes to shield them from the blinding light.

Whitlow set that lamp on the warden's bedside table. "No. It's got to be done tonight. I want them to take care of two women."

The fat warden knuckled the sleep out of his eyes. "Jeezus, women? Which ones?"

"The Hastings widow and a busybody named Miss Starbuck. The Starbuck woman is getting drunk and then laid tonight by Beard. But the Hastings woman is alone at her house. You know the place."

"Well, sure I do, but . . . dammit, there must be some better way than this! I don't like the idea of strangling young women."

"Young or old, what the hell is the difference? Either way, these two women can get us both hanged. I tell you, we got to get rid of them and do it now."

The warden cursed. "All right. I'll get Montoya and Logman up and send 'em out the back way. But

175

they might not like the idea of doing it to a woman any better than I do."

The sheriff bristled. "What the hell is going on here! You've all killed before. I'm the one that got you this job. Is everyone in Yuma going squeamish on me tonight?"

"Take it easy. Take it easy. I said I'd do it. It's just that Logman and Montoya won't like it one damn bit, especially when they see how pretty Mrs. Hastings is."

"Yeah, well, then, tell them to have their pleasure with her before they strangle her. I'll bet that will make the deal sweeter."

"It will," the warden nodded. "It sure as hell will."

Jess Whitlow started to turn on his heel, but checked himself and said, "I tell you one thing, I'm beginning to worry about Beard. This Starbuck woman was eavesdropping on us earlier today, and she knows what's going on and still . . . the love-sick fool is taking her to dinner! If we don't take care of things, we could all go down together because of Beard."

"He's a damn smart man," the warden argued.

"Not when his brains have slipped below his belt, he ain't."

"We'll take care of it," the warden said. "But you're going to have to deal with Beard. When he finds out you acted without his orders, there's going to be hell to pay."

The sheriff balled his fists at his sides. "I tell you something, I'm beginning to think that I'm better qualified to be the first governor of Arizona than Arnold Beard. And I don't give a damn what he's promised us after he's elected, things aren't going at all like they were supposed to go. Hell, the big real estate killing we were supposed to have in Tucson all went up in smoke, and now we got this Starbuck woman just waiting to bring us all down."

The warden pulled on his trousers. "Maybe you're right," he said nervously. "Maybe we should get the hell out of Yuma before it's too late."

"How? The roads are blocked. It was a miracle that we got one man through from Tucson to warn us of what happened to Miller and Turner. I say we stick and we cut Arnold Beard right out of the picture."

"You mean . . ."

"Yeah," the sheriff said. "I'm thinking that after Logman and Montoya finish with the Hastings woman, they ought to go by and pay Arnold and Miss Starbuck a house call. They'd catch them in bed and who knows, after Arnold is killed, I might even join them in having a little taste of Miss Starbuck before we kill her."

"Do you realize that we are talking about killing three people in one night!"

"Three or ten, what's the damn difference? I'm the sheriff, ain't I? I'll make a big fuss of it and put on the greatest acting job Yuma has ever seen. They'll be an investigation. Maybe I'll even kill a town drunk or someone and get the credit for ending the stranglings once and for all. With that kind of publicity, I might even become the leading candidate for the first governor of Arizona."

"And what about me?"

"You'll get a plum job at high pay and a fat pension."

"We'll still have to kill Logman and Montoya in order to wrap up the loose ends."

The sheriff nodded. "If you ever get your fat ass out the door, maybe we can wrap it all up tonight."

The sheriff licked his lips nervously, but he smiled and then he hurried out toward the cells to release the Arizona Stranglers.

Chapter 16

Cassandra Hastings sat across from the young army doctor and said, "Would you like any more tea?"

"No, thank you."

"It's awfully nice of you to come here and keep me company, though I really don't feel I'm in much danger. Jessica is the one taking all the chances."

"I have a feeling this will all be over soon," the lieutenant said, placing his teacup and saucer down. "Tell me, Mrs. Hastings, do you like Yuma?"

"What an odd question." Cassandra smiled. "In truth, I used to hate this desert country, but now I've come to appreciate its own special kind of beauty. But if I had my choice, then I think I'd prefer to live in California."

"What a coincidence," the lieutenant said. "So would I!"

"Then you don't intend to remain in the army?"

"No," he said. "I have enjoyed my enlistment,

but it is almost finished. When it's over, I'm leaving Yuma. Perhaps we might even leave for California together?''

Cassandra blushed. "You're very bold to suggest such a thing. What about Miss Starbuck?"

It was the lieutenant's turn to blush. "I guess not much goes on in this town that escapes the eye. Actually, Jessie has always made it very clear that, when this strangling business is finished, she is returning to her Circle Star Ranch in Texas."

"Without you?"

"Of course," he said. "I have my career, she has hers."

Cassandra nodded her head. "I see."

"Do you?" Jason came over to her side. "I was a great admirer of your late husband, Cassandra. So much so that after he died, well, I never really felt that I measured up to the kind of man that you might consider Warren's equal. So I stayed away and admired you from a distance."

Cassandra swallowed. "Really, Jason, I think . . ."

"No," he said, "please let me finish. I've wanted to say this for a long, long time. I will never be your late husband's equal, and it was foolish of me to even try. What I am is different. But like Warren, I know that I could love you."

Cassandra looked into the young army doctor's eyes. "This is all happening so fast," she said. "Perhaps, after we have seen the end to this intrigue and my late husband's murder has been brought to justice . . . then you and I can talk and even make plans."

Jason grinned. "I could not have expected more and—"

He froze and his voice died in mid-sentence.

"What's wrong?"

"Did you hear a noise behind your house?"

Cassandra shook her head, and they both listened intently for a full minute.

The lieutenant finally relaxed. "I must be hearing things."

"Maybe we should go out on the front porch and look around."

The lieutenant unbuttoned his holster and drew his service revolver. "Someone is out by the back step," he whispered.

Cassandra rushed over to her husband's rolltop desk and drew out a derringer. Warren Hastings had not been the kind of man who enjoyed handling or shooting guns and this was the only one that he had owned. It was a .41 caliber Remington, and her husband had insisted that she become adept at loading and firing the small but powerful weapon.

Cassandra took two extra bullets and clenched them in her left fist while she held the gun in her right. Meanwhile, the lieutenant tiptoed over to the kerosene lamp and extinguished it, plunging the parlor into what would have been absolute darkness if not for the moonlight filtering through a set of big windows.

The lieutenant moved silently back to Cassandra and whispered, "Whoever is coming is at your back door. Is it locked?"

"Of course."

"That won't stop the Arizona Strangler."

The lieutenant placed his hand on Cassandra's shoulder. "Listen, I'm going to take you down the hall and out to the front porch. If I stop the man coming after you, then I'll call out when it is safe to come back inside. But if I don't . . . you run!"

"And leave you . . ."

Lieutenant Caldwell's voice was insistent. "Cassandra, please. Don't argue. It really could be the strangler!"

Cassandra nodded, and with derringer firmly in

hand, she and the lieutenant moved silently down the hall to the front door. Cassandra pushed it open very slowly and stepped out onto the porch. They both heard the back door creak in protest and then the sound of the door closing.

The lieutenant drew the woman close and whispered in her ear. "Stay right here until the shooting is over. If I don't call, then run for your life!"

Cassandra threw her arm around the lieutenant and kissed his mouth before whispering, "I'll go with you to California; just be careful!"

Jason nodded and reentered the hallway. He was a doctor, not a gunfighter, and the idea of taking a human life was totally against his philosophy. If he could, he'd wound the man and then tie him up and bandage the gunshot. Yes, he thought, that is what I'll do. Shoot to wound.

But outside on the front porch, Cassandra Hastings had an entirely different attitude. If the lieutenant did not call, so help her, she was going back inside and she'd shoot to kill. She would rather die than allow the Arizona Strangler to murder both her late husband and the man she hoped would be her future husband.

She was standing by the door listening to her own heartbeat when suddenly she heard the front porch creak. She started to whirl around but felt terrible pain as her breath was cut off and her throat felt as if it had been slit.

Terror flooded her mind and she tried to scream, but the only sound she could make was a dying gurgle. With her mind unraveling, she twisted her derringer around behind her back and pulled the trigger.

The effect was instantaneous. The strangler dropped his arms and staggered backward. He struck the porch rail and clawed at his groin, where Cassandra's bullet had entered. Cassandra heard shots in the hallway. Her throat was on fire and she could barely

181

breathe, but somehow she managed to reload just as the man she had shot sat down on her porch rail and pulled his gun. Cassandra shot first, and the man flipped over backward and crashed into her rose bed.

When she bolted back inside, the lieutenant was struggling for his life with a tall man. The light was so poor that Cassandra could not tell who was winning, so she stood almost paralyzed with fear until she heard the same terrible gurgle that had come from her own throat.

"Jason!" she screamed, fumbling to reload her third bullet. But she dropped the bullet and heard it roll across the wooden floor, lost in the darkness. With a cry of frustration, she flung herself blindly at the two dark silhouettes.

Her attack caught the strangler off balance, and he fell hard. Cassandra, empty derringer still in her hand, slashed blindly knowing that she had nothing to lose and that Jason was being choked to death. The strangler grunted with pain, and Cassandra struck again and again. And then suddenly the strangler jumped up and went racing down the hall.

Cassandra heard the back door slam against the wall and then there was silence.

"Jason? Jason!"

The doctor coughed and began to choke. Cassandra jumped up and ran to the parlor where it seemed to take her forever to find and light a lamp. When she did return to the hall, she almost dropped the lamp, so great was the shock of seeing the army doctor holding his badly bruised throat and trying to get his breath.

Cassandra did not know what to do except to fold to her knees beside the man and hold him close until, finally, he began to breathe normally. After a few more minutes the doctor picked up his army revolver and they helped each other outside.

"I shot a man," Cassandra croaked. "He's lying in my rose garden."

"Get the lamp," Jason wheezed.

When Cassandra brought it outside, Jason used it to illuminate the dead man lying face up in the rose garden. "Oscar Montoya," Jason said. "And I'd bet anything that the man you wounded inside was Art Logman. Come on, we've got to find and warn Jessie!"

Already, people were coming out of their homes wondering what in the world was going on. A neighbor shouted, "Look, there's someone dead in Mrs. Hastings's rose garden!"

As the neighbors hurried over to stare at the dead strangler, Cassandra and the doctor escaped in the confusion.

"Where are we going!"

"To Beard's place," the doctor gasped, knowing that, if he were not too late to help Jessie, he would shoot to kill this time. "Cassandra, we finally know who they are now!"

Two blocks away Art Logman staggered up the street until he came to Arnold Beard's huge mansion. His hat was missing and his scalp was badly lacerated from the pistol-whipping he had just suffered. Blood was running down his face and his wounded leg. Logman was not a man to panic but he could not help wondering what had happened to Oscar Montoya, his accomplice in so many stranglings. Most likely, Oscar was dead. All that Logman was certain of was that someone had been waiting for him in the hallway and he'd barely managed to get his rope around their neck. Even wounded, he'd have strangled his opponent to death, and he vividly remembered hearing the familiar death rattle, but then someone else had rushed in and started pistol-whipping him in the darkness.

Logman cursed his bad luck. The sheriff was expecting him and they were supposed to kill Arnold Beard but if . . .

"Psssst! Over here!"

Logman hobbled over to the sheriff, who stared at him and then cursed. "Jeezus, what the hell happened to you! Where's Montoya!"

"I don't know. Maybe dead, maybe on his way back to the prison. I tell you, I just don't know!"

Sheriff Jess Whitlow shook his head and swore. "Get the hell out of here! You're no use to me anymore."

"But—"

"Go on back to the prison!"

Logman nodded, turned, and ran. He had not taken three steps when the sheriff, knowing that he could not afford to take any chances on a lifer from the Yuma Prison turning on him, drew his knife and hurled it end over end to strike and drive deep into Logman's back.

The sheriff had the feeling that Montoya was dead, and now he knew for certain that Logman was also finished. That meant that only Arnold Beard and the warden could squeal and put his neck in a noose. And right now Arnold Beard was probably alone and in bed with Jessica Starbuck. The sheriff opened the front gate and started up the walk. It was going to be a bloody night, but if he played his cards right and made some kind of phoney arrest, then . . .

"Sheriff!"

Jess Whitlow froze, then slowly turned to see the army doctor and Mrs. Hastings running past Logman's body. The sheriff went for his gun, but before it cleared leather, the doctor stopped, threw out his arm and knocked Cassandra aside and then opened fire. His first wild shot was high, but then the lieutenant, remembering the advice of his army instructors who'd made him take mandatory target practice,

184

squeezed off his next two shots and Sheriff Jess Whitlow took a slug in the shoulder and another through the right lung. He spun around, and when he struck the earth, he found he could not move.

The army doctor was at his side in an instant. He rolled the man over and saw the two ugly wounds, then said, "Sheriff, you might as well talk. I can't do a thing to save you."

"Go . . . go to hell!" Sheriff Whitlow choked just before he died.

Upstairs in his bedroom, Arnold Beard stood fully dressed and leaning out his window looking down on the scene below. Without turning to face Jessie, he said, "The sheriff killed Art Logman and then was shot by the doctor. They're both dead."

He turned to look at Jessie and his face was slack and expressionless. In one hand he held half a bottle of champagne, in the other a gun. Jessie stood with her back to his closet door, her own derringer pointed at the attorney's heart.

"Drop both your gun and the champagne," she said. "The party is over."

Arnold Beard snickered. "I doubt very much that there's anyone left alive that can testify against me. I think I'm going to go scot-free." He giggled. "I haven't done a damn thing wrong that you can prove!"

"Why did you have all those stranglings done in the first place?" Jessie asked.

"Money and power," the man said with a shrug of his shoulders. "I showed you where the money all went. Look around, it's in every piece of furniture, in every painting. Even in this champagne. And power? Well, of course I fully intended to be governor. Now and then, someone like Warren Hastings or Judge Hale in Tucson would catch on to what we were up to. When they couldn't be bought

185

or framed, there was no choice but to eliminate them."

"It's over," Jessie said, her voice shaking with fury. It was all she could do to keep from pulling the trigger.

"Sure it's over," he said. "I can live with that. I'll keep my money, and even though my reputation will be ruined in this territory, I can find another."

"Not from Yuma Prison," Jessie said. "Your fat, corrupt warden will sing like a bird, and he'll either put your neck in a noose or he'll send the both of you to prison for the rest of your lives."

Beard sat down on his windowsill and hoisted his bottle. He drank deeply and eyed Jessie with a mixture of hate and admiration. "At least I got you into my bedroom."

"I'd have rather slept with a dog than you," she said. "Now, drop the gun and the bottle."

He giggled and raised his gun so that it was up beside his face and pointing at the ceiling. "Let's make a deal. I'll give you all my treasures. The paintings, the Oriental rugs, the priceless antiques. Everything, if you'll let me go."

"Not a chance," Jessie said.

Beard took one long, last shuddering gulp of the champagne and then he smiled loosely and said, "In that case, you're going to have to kill me, Miss Starbuck, because I'm not going to hang *or* go to prison."

He dropped the empty bottle, and it rolled noisily across the polished hardwood floor as the barrel of his pistol inched downward and started to come level on Jessie's chest.

Jessie knew she had no choice but to fire. Knew that she either killed this man and robbed the Arizona Territory of courtroom justice or else she was a dead woman.

With deep regret, she fired and . . . through her gunsmoke, she saw Arnold Beard disappear out the second-story window.

Watch for

**LONE STAR AND THE
SHADOW CATCHER**

eighty-eighth novel in the exciting
LONE STAR
series from Jove

coming in December!